Then What Happened?

JOHN ALBERT

ISBN-13: 978-1-7939-5892-1

D edicated to my family. First and foremost, my dear wife, Ann, who has been my greatest support over the years. Her encouragement and love have sustained me. She continues to be the sounding board for all of my crazy ideas and even crazier story lines.

T o my children, you are probably as familiar with these stories as I am. We have discussed them over the years. Thanks for humoring me. You were the motivation, whether you knew it or not, for me to compile these stories. I wanted to pass them on to you; then on to my grandchildren. The cover of this book says it all. They are gathered around me as I tell them a story. Perhaps, one day, these stories will give them a small glimpse into their Papaw's alter ego(s).

T o my extended family: my multitude of cousins, aunts, uncles, nephews, and nieces. These are your stories too. I hope you enjoy my telling of "the bear story". I hope it takes you back to all the wonderful times we shared together.

T o my dear friends. Thank you for letting me share my stories with you; for being gracious and encouraging. For giving me the courage to let my inner world come to light. It is an intimidating thing to open your soul to the public. Your kind words and gentle spirits have lifted me up more than you will ever know.

I hope you all enjoy this eclectic compilation. I look forward to dialoguing with you about it. With the exception of two stories, they are all works of fiction. "The Bear Story" and "A Dog Named Lucky" are true accounts from my childhood. I also included two micro stories: "Eat Your Peas" and "Terror". I finished this collection with three poems that I wrote many years ago. I think they speak to the journey I've been on. I hope they resonate with you.

TABLE OF CONTENTS

Rip Van Winkle Climbed Down a Hole

"When I was a child, I spoke as a child, I understood as a child,
I thought as a child; but when I became a man,
I put away childish things."
Saint Paul, I Corinthians 13:11

Tyler Jenkins knew he probably shouldn't stick his head into a dark hole, but something about being eleven just sort of cancels out that type of thinking. Who would care if something happened to him anyway? Not his parents. And definitely not his sister or his back-stabbing friend Micah. He still couldn't believe that Micah left him to go sit with Sarah during lunch. Heck, they both agreed that Sarah was *his* girl. Micah knew that, and still, he broke all the rules of pre-teen etiquette. *Bros before hoes*, everyone knew that. Tyler would be the first to admit, however, that Sarah probably wasn't a *hoe*. Truth be told, he wasn't completely sure what constituted a "hoe". And, given the chance, he would have done the exact same thing as Micah. Still, that didn't make it right.

Tyler laid on the ground and slowly stuck his head down into the hole. It was hella-dark. *Can't see shit,* he thought. He felt a cool breeze rush across his face. That told him this hole was a lot deeper than it appeared. His mind raced, *Could be a cave!* Even though he was eleven, which meant he was practically a teenager—nearly grown, Tyler could still let himself daydream about pirates and aliens from time to time. This was one of those times. *Maybe it's a cave. Maybe somebody buried treasure in it,* he thought. "Yeah and maybe shit floats!" he said out loud before realizing that shit does, indeed, float. He shrugged his shoulders. Didn't matter anyway, not right now anyhow. He'd have to get back home before dark. He could come back tomorrow. He would need to remember to bring a flashlight. Maybe he'd invite his back-stabbing friend Micah. *If he's not boinkin' Sarah!* he thought. This caused him to wonder what actually constituted *boinkin'*.

Tyler stood up and dusted the dirt from his knees. He froze in absolute shock and disbelief at what he saw. Hoping nobody else was there to hear him and then not really caring he slowly said, "What the fuck?" His mind was whirling. *How in the world?* he thought. He didn't know whether he was scared or confused, maybe a little of both. Tyler was surrounded by the eerie darkness of the woods. He started to panic, and then he remembered his mom. "Holy Shit!" he said as he looked at his wristwatch. "Seven o'clock! That's not friggin' possible!" he screamed to the silent woods. "Shit," he said, as he turned to run back down the trail to his bike. He had to pedal as fast as he could. He had to get home quick. He cursed the darkness. He wished he had brought that damn flashlight. Then he thought, *Who brings a friggin flashlight in the middle of the day anyway?*

He pumped the pedals on his worn-out Schwinn for all they were worth. Tyler played back the afternoon in his mind, trying to figure out what the hell happened. *How the hell can it be dark?* he wondered. "Ok," he said, as he gasped air into his lungs. He started to tick off his afternoon. "I got off the bus at around three-thirty. Threw my shit on the sofa. Had a PB&J. Mom said something about homework and I got on the computer." He racked his brain trying to retrace his steps. "Only like ten maybe fifteen minutes max," he said. "My stupid sister was hogging the TV so I told Mom I was gonna go ride my bike." He paused to let that set in. *That was like four, at the latest,* he thought. "Yeah, cuz Mom said, 'You be home by five Mister Man cuz you need to clean up for supper. Plus I KNOW you have homework.' " He said in his best Mom voice. He looked back at his watch. "So how in the hell is it seven-fifteen?" he asked.

"OK, I farted around the neighborhood for a few minutes then went straight out to Logan's Point," he nodded in agreement with his recollection. "That's what, maybe fifteen minutes? Twenty at the most." He had to come up with a pretty good excuse and pretty damn quick—his Mom was going to be royally pissed. "I started throwing rocks at pinecones," he continued. Tyler remembered knocking a couple of them down, all the while wishing a dumbass squirrel would have shown up. Then he remembered that last rock he threw. He totally missed the pinecone. He watched the rock sail off into the woods like so many of its brothers. This one, however, was different. Instead of a whispered thud marking the end of its flying days, there was a hollow clang that bounced back towards him. *Bounced?* he asked himself and then said, "Yeah, bounced." A sound like that demanded a full investigation. He trudged through the bushes, expecting to find an old car or a case full of money— *a kid can dream, right?* Instead, all he found was a lousy hole in the ground.

Just a hole. Nothing spectacular about it. About the size of a drainage pipe; which is exactly what he thought it was—at first. As he got closer, he upgraded his assessment from pipe to bear hole. *Do bears live in holes?* he wondered. He stood over the hole and looked into it. No way to tell how deep it was. He wished he had another rock to drop down it. He turned back to look at the trail. *Maybe I should go get a rock*, he thought. *Nah, I'll check it out first*, he countered.

Tyler stopped and did some more quick mental calculations. "OK, so I'm at the trail no later than four-thirty. Then I go to the hole. That was only like two or three more minutes. Then all I did was lay down and stick my face in that stupid thing for maybe ten seconds." Tyler racked his brain. He had to be forgetting something. How else could he explain sticking his face in a hole at four-thirty and standing up at seven? He was frantic for an explanation. "Maybe I passed out," he said. That would explain the time difference. Then he remembered thinking about the possibility of buried treasure and saying out loud something about the buoyancy of feces. *Definitely wasn't passed out,* he thought. What then? What could it possibly be? How could two and a half hours pass in less than ten seconds?

It didn't matter now. He looked up and breathed a gritted, "Shit" through his teeth. He was home. Worse than that, his mom was standing on the front porch with a phone in one hand and her wrinkled apron in the other. He threw his bike down in a heap and started up the steps.

"You better have a good explanation!" his mom said. Her words were simmering. What hurt Tyler the most was the pain he felt in them. He saw the tears and the worried expression in her eyes. She put one hand on her hip and the other right into his chest. "Well?" she demanded.

Tyler said the first thing that came to his mind. He knew it wasn't true but what else could he say other than, "I fell asleep." He added as an afterthought, "I'm sorry." It seemed to appease her.

The next day, during lunch, Tyler slid his government sanctioned peas from one side of the tray to the other. His mind was still stuck on yesterday's mystery. Try as he might, he could not come up with a satisfactory explanation as to what happened to his entire afternoon. Lost in his thoughts, he didn't notice Micah step in front of him. "What 'cha doing dipshit?" Micah asked as he plopped down across from Tyler. He grimaced at his "friend's" intrusion.

"Where's your *girlfriend*?" Tyler asked.

"You talking about Sarah," Micah asked as though he was completely clueless.

"Duh. Dickweed. Who else?" Tyler asked.

"Ah, she likes that Mexican kid."

"Jesse?"

"Yeah. She said they were going to the park or some shit," Micah said as he lit into his mashed potatoes.

For reasons he couldn't completely fathom, Tyler was excited about this new development. Out of the blue he said, "Well I can't speak Spanish anyway!" This brought such a deep laugh from Micah that he actually spit up some of mashed potatoes. Together they both started squealing out loud in their best "Speedy Gonzales" accent, while fist-pumping the air, "Arriba! Arriba!" And that was that. The *Bros* were *Bros* again. Deep down, however, Tyler imagined that this wouldn't be the last

4

time they were separated by a girl. He was right about that.

Tyler waited all week for Saturday to get here. He wanted to check that hole out again, but was afraid to have a repeat of his last adventure—especially on a school night. Saturdays were his. Between breakfast and supper nobody wondered where he was or what he was doing. The perfect scenario for exploration! This time, however, he wouldn't be alone.

Micah knocked on the front door at precisely nine-forty-seven a.m. Tyler answered with a backwards holler to his Mom, "Bye Mom, we're gonna go riding." He was thankful that was all the explanation she asked for on a Saturday. He already knew what she was going to say in response and here it came on cue, "You be safe and be back home for supper."

"Sure Mom," he said, as he shut the front door and headed off towards a rapidly changing future.

"So what's the big friggin mystery Sherlock?" Micah asked.

"Just wait," Tyler said. He was already feeling foolish for bringing Micah along. He should have checked it out further before inviting him. He started to, but then thought, *Hell, worst case scenario we just stick our heads into a hole.* To which he quickly added, *Wouldn't be the first time.*

As they mounted their bikes Tyler asked Micah, "So how much time you got? When are your folks expecting you back?"

Micah gave him a WTF look. "It's Saturday asshole," he said. "All they care about is me staying out of their way all day long." Then he added, "You know that. No different than any other friggin' weekend."

Tyler thought, as they pedaled to Logan's Point, *OK, if it's all just bullshit, it won't matter.* After all, they were pre-teen boys, and as any pre-teen boy can testify: checking out a deep, dark hole is an adventure in and of itself.

As they stood over the unimpressive hole, Micah was the first to break the silence, "So this is it? You brought me out here for a friggin' hole?" On the inside, however, he was imaging all of the fantastic implications—and yes, pirates and buried treasure also entered his pre-pubescent mind. He couldn't just say it out loud though. He and Tyler had entered that dreaded realm of no-man's land. Somewhere between boy and man. Neither one wanted to admit which side they stood on at any particular moment. Once, however, the other intimated they were on the same side they would quickly abandon themselves to the moment.

He waited for some clue as to how Tyler was approaching the moment. He was relieved when Tyler said, "I don't know, I was just thinking it was pretty cool, that's all. You know, anything could be down there."

Micah took a chance, "Yeah, could be anything; hell, some gangsters could've stashed some shit in there." He looked back at Tyler. He was shaking his head in agreement. They both knew the drill. "Hell could be anything," he said and then added cautiously, "Or nothing." They both nodded in agreement. However, in their hearts, they both dreamed of unimaginable things waiting in the depths of the hole.

"So what's the plan?" Micah asked.

Tyler kept his own plan secret and said, "Let's drop a rock in it and see how deep it is!"

Micah scurried for a good sized rock and soon held it over the rim of the hole. "Let 'er rip!" Tyler said as Micah released it. They both leaned forward to hear and were surprised by the sound that bounced out of the hole.

"What the hell was that?" Micah asked as a reverberating metallic twang echoed back up at them.

Tyler quickly responded, "That's what I'm talking about. What the hell is that?" He suddenly felt justified in bringing his friend in on the expedition.

"So how deep is this bitch?" Micah asked.

It was now time for Tyler's private experiment. Nothing ventured, nothing gained, as they say. He told Micah, "Let's shine a light down it and see." Micah quickly agreed.

He handed Micah the light. They both laid on the ground. In his most NASA sounding voice Tyler glanced at his watch and said, "Exploration commencing at precisely ten-twenty-three a.m."

"You are such a friggin' dweeb Tyler!" Micah said as he flicked on the light.

That's alright, Tyler thought, *it might be bullshit, but now we'll know for sure.*

Laying on their stomachs, they both peered over the edge of the hole. Again, Tyler felt that cool breeze brush across his face. Micah panned the light around the edges of the hole. It definitely appeared man-made. The sides were smooth with an almost glass-like quality. It almost looked like a laser could have drilled the hole—assuming, of course, there was a laser capable of doing such a thing. In the minds of two eleven year old boys, anything was possible. Micah finally broke the silence, "I wonder who made this?"

Tyler was too preoccupied to answer. He was silently counting to twenty. *No more than twenty,* he told himself. He was at eleven when Micah said, "What the hell is that?"

He saw it too—at the bottom of the hole. "Hold the friggin' light still!" he screamed at Micah. *What the hell is that?* He wondered. He strained to make it out as the seconds ticked by. They both leaned in further. They could just make out a round shape at the bottom of the hole. Which, as far as he could tell, looked to be about fifteen feet deep. A deeply pitted sphere was half-buried in the bottom of the hole. It was about the size of a basketball. Which is exactly what they would've guessed it to be except for one thing. The light *wobbled* around it. No other way to explain it, the light wobbled. It was as though the sphere was pulling the light into itself. The closer the light got to the sphere the more it wobbled and flickered different colors. Tyler immediately thought of the Northern Lights they studied in Science class. It was like that, only on a much smaller scale. He could hear Micah mumbling something beside him. He continued counting in his mind: *fifteen Mississippi; sixteen Mississippi; seventeen Missi....* Tyler scanned the bottom of the hole in a panic. *Where's the rock?* Seconds ticked by as he scanned the small space for it. Nothing. Finally he hollered out loud, "Where's the damn rock?" It was nowhere to be seen.

Micah, who was lost in his own thoughts, said, "Dude, is that thing alive?"

Tyler strained to get a better look. The words, *"twenty Mississippi"*, bounced around inside his head. *What does that even mean?* he wondered. *Stand up!* his mind screamed, *Stand up!* It shook him out of his trance. He suddenly remembered why they were there and what they were doing. He shouted, "UP! STAND UP!"

Micah obeyed, not really knowing why, and said, "What the hell, dildo?"

Tyler took a deep breath to steady his nerves. He could already feel the change. He knew he was right. The woods confirmed it. "How long?" he asked.

"What?" Micah asked.

Tyler scanned the woods and asked again, "How long? How long were we looking in the hole?"

Micah looked confused. "What kinda dumbass question is that? We just stuck our heads in there."

"How long?" Tyler asked again

"Hell, I don't know. Thirty seconds at the most. What the fuck difference does it make?" Micah asked. Even as he asked the question he could sense that something had changed in the universe. The world had shifted forward somehow.

"Because," Tyler said, glancing at his watch. "Do you remember what time it was when we looked into the hole?"

"What is this, Jeopardy?" Micah asked.

"What time, Micah?" Tyler asked. "What time did I say it was?"

Micah thought, "Uh, Ten-twenty-three. You said some shit about it being ten-twenty-three. Who gives a rat's ass?"

"Look at what time it is now, dipshit!" Tyler said as he thrust his hand towards Micah.

Micah glanced down and saw the hands on Tyler's watch proudly displaying the current time of four-fifty-two. He grabbed Tyler's hand and pulled in for a closer look. He scrutinized the hands on the watch. No way to deny it. They were pointing to four-fifty-two. His mind scurried for an explanation. Then it hit him, "Yeah, real funny Tyler! You think I'm that stupid? You just changed the time of your watch while we were looking in that hole!"

Tyler grabbed Micah by the shoulder. "Look around you asshole! You think I changed that?"

Micah looked around the woods. There was no denying it. Morning had given way to afternoon. Soft shadows were falling across the branches. The sun had traveled to the far edge of the sky. Time had shifted. The universe had move forward without them.

Reality slowly dawned on Micah. "Oh, shit!" he said. "If it really is four-fifty-two that means we only got like eight minutes to get home before our Moms start going ape-shit on us!" Tyler agreed. Quantum physics and mysteries of the universe aside, neither of them wanted to deal with a pissed-off mom.

They pedaled for all they were worth back to Tyler's house. As soon as they stepped inside, Tyler's mom glanced at the clock. Five o'clock on the money. They were safe. Micah promptly called home and begged permission to spend the night. He held the phone out and Tyler's mom said, "Its fine with me Marsha. They're in for the night and Micah can just borrow some of Tyler's PJ's. We'll send him back home after breakfast."

"You boys wanna watch the movie?" Tyler's dad asked as they both started up the stairs after supper. They looked at each other and mirrored an imperceptible "no" with their eyes.

"No Sir," Tyler said as he and Micah turned to run up the stairs.

"What's the rush?" his dad asked.

"Uh," Tyler thought, "We've got a science project we want to do some browsing on."

His sister chimed in from the sofa, "More like a biology project I bet!"

Tyler stuck out his teeth in a classic, slack-jawed mule impression and chortled, "Ga-haw, Ga-haw. Real funny Sis."

His dad stared at him intently. His eyes drilled the unspoken threat that he knew Tyler understood what would happen if he went to those web sites he had been repeatedly warned about. "Science," he said, and then added, "I'll be up to check on you in a bit."

Tyler said, "Yes Sir," knowing full well that his dad would not be checking in on him—he never did. Still, he would lock his bedroom door just to be sure.

Micah sat on the bed. "OK. I'll say it," and then he did, "Whiskey Tango Foxtrot?"

"I don't know," Tyler said. "I was thinking maybe it was fumes or something, you know?" He looked at Micah for reassurance.

"Fumes?"

10

"Yeah, like maybe we were high or passed out?" Even as he said it he knew it was bullshit.

"No way. We talked the whole time. Plus, we were steadily shining the light around," Micah said, his thoughts far away. "No. It was that thing in the hole. That thing did it."

"What the hell was it?" Tyler asked.

They both huddled around the computer as Tyler began searching for, "things that make time stand still". Micah punched his arm, "Seriously? That's what you're searching for?"

"You got a better idea?" Knowing he didn't, Tyler hit the enter button.

After thirty minutes of following dead end links and sites, Tyler pushed the keyboard away and said, "Nothing? Nothing on the frigging internet about time standing still? You gotta be kidding me!"

"Who cares anyway?" Micah asked. His ADD had kicked in twenty minutes ago. It was obvious that Tyler, visibly frustrated, didn't share his sentiment.

"Who cares?" Tyler asked. "I care. I mean, come on, this is some freaky shit, right?"

Micah shrugged, "Yeah, but so what? I mean what difference does it make?" He could tell that Tyler wasn't on board. He added, "I mean how much fun is a friggin' hole that slows time down?" Micah fell back on the bed. "Now if that bitch could speed time up—like a time machine...now THAT would be cool!" He laid there for a moment and sat up with an inspiring thought, "Could you imagine, pop down in that hole one day and then come out like twenty or maybe a hundred years in the future. How sweet would that be?"

Tyler wanted to join in on this new fantasy, but instead shook his head and said, "Yeah, everybody we know would be dead. How sweet would that be?"

Micah said, with a distant look in his eyes, "Might not be that bad."

The boys sat there in silence pondering the matter. Something was nagging Tyler. It was eating at the edges of his brain. Finally, it hit him. He jumped up and said, "It does!"

"It does what?" Micah asked.

Tyler was pacing the floor. "Don't you see? That's exactly what it does dipshit! The hole speeds time up!"

"Bullshit," Micah said, "It slows it down. That's what happened to us remember," and then added with emphasis, "DIPSHIT!"

"No. No. No." Tyler said shaking his head. He turned and faced his friend. "It slows time down INSIDE the hole. Think about it." He waited for Micah to connect the dots. "Don't you see? OUTSIDE the hole time DOES speed up! That's exactly what happened to us. Think about it Micah."

Micah, a solid C+ student, tried to process what Tyler was saying. He just shook his head. "Not seeing it Dude."

"Look", Tyler explained, "We stuck our head in that hole for like thirty seconds, right?" Micah shook his head in agreement. "And then when we stood up and half the day was gone, right?" He waited for Micah to catch up. It took a few seconds.

Micah jumped to his feet. "That's right!" Now he started pacing. "That's right!" He pointed his finger at Tyler in a jabbing motion and declared, "Time goes faster OUTSIDE the hole. A hell of a lot faster!"

Again, Tyler made his slack-jaw impression and said, "Duh, dumbass. That's what I'm saying."

They both stared ahead silently. Micah eventually broke the silence,

"So now what?"

Tyler answered, "Now what?" He placed his hand on Micah's shoulder, "Now, we have a time machine."

A sense of awe overcame the both of them. "A time machine," Micah said, "A friggin' time machine."

Tyler's brain was whirling. "Yeah. We just gotta figure out how to use it."

The next week drug by as the boys spent every free moment talking about their discovery. On Friday, during lunch, Micah said, "I been thinking."

"That's new and different," Tyler said. He glanced up in time to see Micah flash him the universal one-finger salute.

"Seriously, I was thinking that we really only have one option with the hole." He looked over at Tyler to see if he had somehow come to the same conclusion.

"Oh yeah, and what might that be?"

"Well, it's like this," he said as he glanced around to make sure nobody else was listening. "If we just pop our head in and out—then BAM we lose another friggin Saturday."

Tyler shook his head as he sipped from his milk carton. "I'm listening."

"And if we stay longer than that—let a day or two pass by, well, all we're gonna get out of that is an ass-beating."

Tyler stared at him. "An ass-beating? Don't tell me your folks still do that shit. Do they?"

Micah averted his eyes. Tyler knew, only too well, the hell that

Micah lived with. His dad was long gone and the latest in a long line of live-in boyfriends was a scumbag of the highest order named Todd. He was an abusive, unemployed alcoholic who dispensed his own brand of discipline while Micah's mom sat by, glued to the TV, high on a mixture of pain pills and red wine. Tyler said, "That's bullshit man." Then he added, "You need to get out of that place; run away or something."

Micah shook his head, "Exactly."

Tyler paused, "Wait. What are you talking about?"

"Like I was saying, we really only got one option. We gotta go whole hog. Go into the hole and stay there."

"Stay there?" Tyler said. "That's insane."

"Not forever, just long enough to get to the future."

Tyler couldn't believe what he was hearing. "The future? What future? We don't have any idea how long we'd need to stay in there…or what we'd be coming out to for that matter." Micah started digging in his pocket for something. Tyler continued, hoping to add a little levity, "Hell we could pop out right in the middle of the Zombie Apocalypse!" He laughed while Micah slid a piece of paper over to him.

"I been doing some figuring," Micah said.

Tyler looked over the paper, "What the hell is this?"

Micah grabbed it back, "Look I ain't the best at math, but still I think this makes sense." He laid the paper down so Tyler could see his computations. "OK, we know we were looking in that hole like thirty seconds right? And then about six hours or so passed outside the hole, agreed?"

Tyler shook his head in agreement. "So," Micah said, "That means that one minute in the hole would equal about twelve hours outside the hole. Am I right?" Tyler thought about it and had to agree. "Alright, so that means if there's twenty four hours in a day," he said as he pointed to his math work, "then you multiply that by two," he pointed at his figures, "and it comes out that every two minutes in the hole is equal to one full day outside the hole." Micah was clearly proud of his formula. He was beaming.

Tyler thought as he looked at his friend, *that must be how Einstein felt with that whole E=MC² thing.* He smiled.

Micah continued, "Alright, this is where it gets tricky." He pointed back to the paper to show his work. "So, there's three-hundred-sixty-five days in a year. We multiply that by the two minutes for each day and it comes out that..." he stopped and looked up at Tyler. "I had to use the calculator for this part." He ran his finger down the paper. "OK, basically it works out that twelve hours in the hole is equal to one year outside the hole. That means every day we stay in the hole, two whole years pass by!"

Tyler pushed the paper away, "You don't know that Micah." He looked at his friend, still not believing what Micah was considering, "You're just guessing."

"Bullshit!" Micah said, "The math works out. Look at it!"

"We have no idea how this works," Tyler said. "Or what it is. You're just guessing."

"Yeah, I know, we ain't got it all figured out. But, what the hell? The math is based on what we do know. You gotta admit that." He waited for Tyler's response.

Tyler grabbed the paper, "OK, even if, and I do mean IF it worked out—how long are you talking about?" Tyler did some quick math in his head, *one day equals two years, so...* "Damn, Micah," he said. "We'd have to stay in that friggin hole ten days for twenty years to pass by! TEN DAYS!" Then he added, as though the thought had not occurred to Micah, "That's ten days in a friggin hole! I am NOT spending ten days in a hole!"

Micah flipped the paper over. "Yeah I know. I did the math too." He looked into his friends eyes. "Look," he said, "I just can't bear the thought of spending the summer with that dipshit Todd in the house every day." There was nothing Tyler could say to that. "So, I was thinking, when school's out for the summer, that maybe I pop in the hole for one hour. Not even an hour." He was pointing to his scribbling on the back of the paper. "See, if two minutes equals one day, then forty minutes would be like eighty days!" He was smiling from ear to ear as he looked at is friend.

"What are you getting at, Micah?" he asked.

"Well, I figure I could spend like forty minutes in that hole and miss the whole damn summer with Todd!"

He couldn't believe what he was hearing. "First off, your math is backwards. Eighty days would take one-hundred-sixty minutes—not forty." Micah grabbed the paper and looked back over his figures. "That's assuming it even works that way," Tyler said.

Micah stuffed the paper back in his pants pocket. He was clearly embarrassed about his error. "So what? That's only a couple of hours," he said. "I'd gladly stay in a friggin hole a couple of hours to escape Todd's bullshit."

Tyler eyed his friend. "You're serious aren't you?" he asked.

Micah shook his head.

"Dude, that's a whole friggin summer down the tubes," Tyler said. He considered the implications and thought, *whole summer of me hanging out with nobody.* "I don't like it," he said.

"It'd be worth it to me," Micah said.

Tyler could see in his friend's eyes that he meant it. He processed it all and said, "My mom would kill me if I skipped out like that."

Micah grunted, "Mine probably won't even notice I'm gone."

And that was that. There was nothing Tyler could do to talk Micah out of his plans. And there was no way in hell he was going to join him. Besides, he had heard that Sarah and Jesse had split up.

Tyler stood beside the hole with Micah. He couldn't believe that summer was here and that his best Bro in the world was going to spend it hiding in a hole. He tried once more, "Dude, are you sure?" He already knew what Micah's answer would be.

"Sure as shit," Micah said, then added, "Friggin Todd's already on a full-blown day-drunk. I hate that asshole!"

"OK," Tyler said, resigned to his friend's decision, "So what's the plan?"

"Again?" Micah asked, "How many times have we been over this?"

"Again," Tyler said, "I want to make sure, that's all."

Micah dropped his back-pack. "OK, I'm only gonna stay in the hole about two and a half hours, right?" He tapped his wristwatch. "No more."

"What's all the shit in the bag for?" Tyler asked. He couldn't hide his suspicion. What if Micah was planning on a full blast to the future? Hoping to see Spock and Captain Kirk on the other side?

Micah opened the bag. "It's just a couple of sandwiches, some chips and sodas," he dug around, "a flashlight, blanket, empty bottle, rope, something to read." He smiled as he held up one of Todd's girly-magazines.

"I know what the reading material is for," Tyler said as he made exaggerated jerking motions with his hand. Micah dropped it back in the bag. "What's the empty bottle for?"

"Uh, to piss in dumbass," Micah said, surprised his friend hadn't

17

thought of that. "Here," he said as he handed the rope to Tyler and pointed, "tie this to that tree."

Micah shouldered the backpack. He handed Tyler a folded piece of paper.

"What's this?"

"The note; remember?"

"Oh yeah, the note." Micah said he was going to write a note telling his folks he was going to Montana to work on a real ranch for the summer. He found it on the internet and had saved up for a roundtrip bus ticket. He knew they wouldn't approve so he just did it. He would be back home in time for school to start. Tyler started reading it. Micah snatched it from him.

"That's not for you!" He refolded it and stuck it in Tyler's shirt pocket. "Just give it to my mom—if she ain't too high to read it." He backed up to the hole, "Like she's gonna care anyway." He looked at Tyler. "OK dipshit, here goes nothing. Remember, don't tell anybody about the hole. Stick with the story. Period." They stared at each other for long time. No words were needed for this moment. It was a good thing too. None came to mind.

Micah looked at his watch, "Alright, two and a half hours to me, end of the summer to you." He smiled and did a two finger salute off his forehead. "Remember, take the rope with you and the day before school starts you drop it back in the hole and help me out. Got it?"

"Yeah I got it, dipshit." Tyler bit his lip. "Are you sure you wanna do this Micah?"

"Sure as shit amigo. Sure as shit." And with that he started his descent into the hole.

Tyler went back to his bike to get his flashlight. When he turned around Micah was nowhere to be seen. He stared at the rope. It was still taut and moving. Micah was climbing down the hole. Something was wrong. His mind was racing to solve a problem that he hadn't even realized was there in the first place. As he got closer to the hole, a thought hit him, "Wait a minute," he said out loud. Then he thought, if time goes slower in the hole, then it should take longer to get to the bottom of the hole. He couldn't get his brain wrapped around it. He started to panic. What if they had it all wrong? What if time went faster inside the hole? His brain was hurting trying to figure it out. Then he remembered the rock that Micah dropped in. They watched it fall. For some reason, his brain was telling him that wasn't right. It should have taken forever to get to the bottom of the hole, right? He wasn't sure at this point. It didn't matter though, because that's not what happened. The rock dropped just like any other rock. It fell at a normal pace. And when it hit the bottom, they heard that weird bouncing sound. He stopped in his tracks. It didn't hit! We didn't see the rock at the bottom! It wasn't there! "What the hell!" he shouted as he ran towards the hole. Just as he got there, the rope went slack. "Son-of-a-bitch!" he hollered out loud.

Tyler flipped on the light and started to lay on the ground when he remembered what happened the last time. Instead, he stood over the hole and pointed the flashlight down into it. The rope was slack against the side of the hole. "Micah!" he hollered into the hole. Nothing. He panned the light around the hole. Micah was gone. Tyler was in full blown panic now. He aimed the beam of light straight down. The dimpled orb pulsed as the light hit it. The light broke into waves around it and wobbled just as before. It was hard to tell if it was pulling the light in or pushing it away. All he knew was that Micah was not in the hole—not that he could see anyway. He didn't know what to do. After about twenty minutes of circling the hole, he grabbed the rope and pulled on it. He hoped that maybe, just maybe, Micah was still hanging on to it, somehow. Nothing. The rope easily pulled up out of the hole.

He stood over the hole with the rope in his hand. Now what? Tyler walked around the hole some more; shining the light from every angle he could and still—nothing! Micah was nowhere to be seen. He sat down to think. "OK," he said out loud. "This changes nothing. I still come back at the end of summer. I drop the rope down and Micah climbs out." He seemed appeased with this. "Yeah, stick with the plan. Nothing changes."

19

He knew in his heart, however, that everything had.

The first three days of Micah's absence was filled with cops and Micah's crying mom. Even Todd seemed to genuinely care. Of course he threatened to beat the living shit out of "Marsha's dumbass kid" as soon as he got back. "Stupid little prick, don't know how good he's got it here." Todd told the cops.

Yeah, Tyler thought, *it's like growing up a Romney.*

No less than two cops and one social worker grilled Tyler for any insight he could offer. He stuck with the story about the ranch in Montana along with the roundtrip bus tickets. The cops did what they could—but they had more pressing issues than a kid chasing a wild-eyed dream. By the fourth day, life returned to normal. Micah's mom went back to her daily regime of pain pills and merlot. Todd weaseled Micah's absence as a way to get himself invited to a couple of neighborhood bar-b-cues. After it was clear that he was only there for the free beer, his invites dried up. Marsha made a couple of appearances on the local news where she gave a heartfelt, albeit, slurred, plea for Micah to come home. APB's with Micah's picture were sent to every precinct in Montana. Nothing came of it. Within two weeks his pictures were covered up or taken down to make room for the latest "missing person" announcement.

Tyler "accidentally" ran into Sarah at the water park twice. The third time it was an official date—his first ever. Sharing a hot dog sealed the deal. Even though there wasn't much that Sarah had in the way of filling out her bikini, still it gave Tyler's young imagination plenty to work with. Many nights he lay awake thinking of her and often awoke, with her still on his mind, to his own personal pup tent the next morning.

Tyler turned twelve that summer. He missed Micah every single day. His mom threw a party and let him invite all of his friends. He thought about Micah hiding in that hole. Hoping he was still there. His thoughts about Micah, however, couldn't compete with the ones he was having about Sarah. While everyone else was in the backyard, he and Sarah snuck into the house. There in the confines of his bedroom he became a man. He kissed a girl for the first time. It wasn't what he thought it would be, but still, it was something. It excited him. He definitely wanted more. He placed his hand on Sarah's side, wondering if he should go for second base. She seemed to know instinctively what he was up to. She smiled her most flirtatious twelve year old smile, turned, kicked one foot behind her in a semi-cheerleader pose and trotted back outside. She waved the cutest little "tootle-doo" as she did. He was smitten; full-on-dead-in-the-face-with-a-sledgehammer-smitten. For a second he thought about Micah. Just for a second. Then he ran back outside to be with Sarah.

Summer came and went in a glorious blur. Tyler eventually did get to second base with Sarah during one eventful swim party. Like his first kiss, it wasn't what he thought it would be, but, like the kiss, he definitely wanted more. He couldn't wait to tell Micah about it. Micah may have girly-magazines, but Tyler had touched "real" boob! Well, as real as a twelve year old girl can offer. He imagined the look on Micah's face when he shared the news. He wondered what he would say. How he would react.

On the last day of summer he stood outside the hole. Even though he brought the flashlight, he was afraid to use it. He was afraid of what he would or what he wouldn't see. He tied the rope to the tree and coiled the rest of it in his hand. He hollered down into the hole as he threw the rope down, "Alright Dipshit! Your two and a half hours are up!"

The rope uncoiled into the hole. He waited for some indication that Micah had picked up the other end of it. Nothing. He jiggled the rope. "Come on Dipshit! Stop whacking off and grab the rope." Nothing. After a few minutes he dropped the rope and flipped on the flashlight. He was dreading this moment. Again, he stood over the hole and shined the light down into it. Nothing. Just that warbling pulse as the light bounced off the object. Tyler panicked. His young brain frantically searched for some answer to the question it kept asking, *"Now what?"*

Tyler paced around the hole hoping that Micah would materialize. The only movement he saw, however, was that damn thing doing its best to suck in the beam from his flashlight. *"How do you turn that thing off?"* Tyler wondered. Finally an idea broke through the surface. "It can't hurt," he said out loud. Tyler ran into the surrounding woods in search of the implement of the only idea he could come up with: a stick. He needed one long enough that he could poke that damn orb with. Maybe it would turn it off. Only one way to find out. It took several minutes of scurrying through the underbrush to come up with a suitable candidate. He drug a small, but straight, dead tree back to the hole.

He tried holding the flashlight in one hand and the tree in the other but that proved too difficult. Tyler laid the flashlight down and grabbed the tree with both hands and let it slide through his hands as he lowered it down into the hole. Thankfully the orb was still pulsing so it gave off just enough light to guide him. Tyler got to the end of the tree and held on. He peered down into the hole. *Too short! Damn it!* Tyler could see the orb still pulsing. The end of the tree dangled about three feet over the top of it. Again, came the earlier question, *Now what?* Tyler went through his options. Laying down and getting his head anywhere near that hole was out. Maybe he could squat and get a little lower? *That's not gonna work*, he thought. So doing the only thing he could think to do, Tyler held the tree firmly in his hands and raised it back up as high as he could. His plan was simple. He would launch it as fast as he could at the orb. "Here goes nothing!" he said out loud. And with that he jabbed the tree down with all of his might. He felt the end of it slide out of his hands towards its intended target. It was a very short journey. A strange bouncing noise let him know the tree had made contact.

He grabbed the flashlight and leaned over the hole. He scanned the hole. *What the hell?* The tree was gone. He shined the light straight at the orb. Something had changed. The orb sat there. No warbling. No pulsing. It just sat there. He leaned over as far as he dared and held the light directly over the top of the orb. *Did I turn it off?* He wondered.

Before he could ponder this latest development the hole exploded with light. A violent force erupted through the hole. Something like warm liquid light blew out of the hole hitting him in the chest with the force of a good-sized linebacker. Tyler felt the wind go out of him as his feet flew off the ground. He was thrown backwards a good ten feet. As his back struck the hard earth, Tyler felt his consciousness slipping away. Darkness rushed all around him. He gasped for air as the darkness consumed him.

Minutes ticked by as Tyler laid motionless on the ground. His eyes fluttered and then flew open. He could not catch his breath. No matter how deeply he tried to gulp in the air it just wouldn't come. His mind flashed back to a baseball game he watched with his dad. A runner, trying to get home had collided full force with the catcher. The runner was sprawled out on the ground, like Tyler, gasping for his next breath. He saw the coach rush over and drop down beside the man. With everyone screaming and hollering he could hear the coach say to him, "Relax. Slow down. Take slow, easy breaths. You'll be alright. Slow, easy breaths."

Slow, easy breaths, his brain echoed. *Slow, easy breaths.* Tyler complied. He relaxed and his breathing returned to normal. *How long was I out?* he wondered. And then, *What the hell happened?* The hole! He sat up. He was sore and would hurt like hell for the next couple of days but nothing seemed broken. He was just about to stand up when he saw something move out of the corner of his eye. The rope! The rope was tight and was slowly moving from side to side. Somebody was climbing up! He stood to his feet. *Son-of-a-bitch!* His back screamed in pain, but that didn't matter. "Micah!" he hollered out loud.

Tyler slowly made his way towards the hole. He could hear labored breathing. "Micah, you asshole! You scared the shit out of me!" He stopped in his tracks. A single hand appeared out of the hole. It was quickly followed by another accompanied with a series of grunts as the climber struggled to rise out of the hole. Tyler felt a wave of relief flood over him. "Oh my God, Micah," he started to say and then stopped in mid-sentence. Something was wrong! It took his brain a few seconds to process what his eyes were seeing. The hands! Something was wrong with the hands. His brain slowly confirmed what his eyes were seeing. Those were NOT the hands of an eleven year old boy. Those were the hands of an old man—a very old man.

The two weathered and worn hands clawed the dirt and grass struggling to find purchase. They dug into the ground as Tyler came closer. He was torn between two decisions: help or run. As he pondered what course of action to take, a head began to rise out of the hole. Tyler stared in confusion. What hair he could see was snow white. The man lurched forward in one final pull. The lower half of his body was still in the hole. He laid on his stomach, completely spent of all energy. Tyler squatted down in front of the old man. He scanned the tattered clothes and the small, frail, old body. There was something very familiar about all of it. The old man raised his head and looked up at Tyler. *The eyes! The face! Oh my God!* He flopped back on the ground.

The old man stared deep into his eyes for several seconds and finally spoke. "You gonna sit there all day Dickweed? Or you gonna help me up?"

-2-

-The Coma Diet-

> "For we that are in this tabernacle do groan,
> being burdened."
> Saint Paul, II Corinthians 5:4

T he Coma Diet, it began as a joke. Now it was a national bestseller. Dr. Jeff Combs had to laugh at his sudden fame, not to mention wealth. He owed it all to the formerly rotund actor, Gavin West.

Gavin's chance encounter with a telephone pole, while driving way too fast and way too drunk, set everything into motion. It took the "Jaws of Life", along with the aid of an improvised tow-truck cable, to extricate his triple-extra-large frame from one very form-fitting sports car. Of course it made the national news. Gavin's flabby body hanging in mid-air looked like a "Save the Whales" training video.

Gavin West would be in a coma for nearly four months. The first glimpse the nation got of Gavin was the day he walked out of the hospital, ninety-seven pounds lighter than when he was wheeled in. The morning gossip columns opined as to whether the accident was just a cover up for a complete make-over of Mr. West.

Jeff Combs was Gavin's attending physician. At the request of the actor's agent, Jeff held a press conference to dispel the rumors. With Perot-like charts he described the coma and the effects it had on Mr. West. Forget the medicine and the science that saved his life, all the press cared about was the weight loss.

25

"Dr. Combs, can you explain how Gavin West lost nearly a hundred pounds while in a coma?"

Jeff smiled, "You can't eat while you're in a coma."

"Are you saying that the hospital starved him?" a member of the press corps shouted.

The Hospital Administrator stood up, "Not at all. I assure you Mr. West received top notch care." He looked at Jeff, "Dr. Combs can explain."

Jeff pointed to a chart, "It's really simple math. A man Mr. West's weight, prior to the accident requires approximately 3,400 calories per day to maintain his weight."

"So what was his starting weight?" a reporter chimed in.

"I'm not at liberty to share that information," *or that he had a tummy tuck and pec implants,* Jeff's inner voice continued.

Jeff pointed to the next chart. "We limited his caloric intake during the coma to 800 calories a day."

"Why so little?" another reporter asked.

"We give the body all it needs to survive, not a calorie more," he answered.

"Is that to cut costs?" the same reporter asked. This brought a few chuckles.

"Actually, it's to cut waste," he answered to even more chuckles. "You can see," Jeff continued, "We reduced Mr. West's intake by 2,600 calories per day." He looked around the press pool. *They are eating this up,* he thought.

"That's a little more than four Happy Meals," the Hospital

Administrator interjected. Laughter filled the room.

"So," Jeff continued, "2,600 calories times 130 days, equals a 338,000 calorie deficit." Jeff tapped the chart for emphasis. "And as you can see, one pound of fat is around 3,500 calories. Do the math and Mr. West loses ninety-seven pounds in four months."

"Thank you, Dr. Combs," the Administrator took the podium. He scanned the crowd of reporters. The man was positively salivating. Jeff shook his head as the Administrator said, "It's a dieter's dream." Cameras flashed. "No Exercise. No hunger. You close your eyes fat and you wake up thin."

That was how it all began. The Administrator pushed him to write a tell-all book about Gavin West and the *Coma Diet*. He even suggested the title, "While You Were Sleeping". Jeff knew the Administrator smelled money. He was right. They had more than they could have imagined. The entire third floor of C-wing serviced their "Coma Diet" clients. The lawyers insisted they not be called patients. Dr. Jeff Combs became the Chief Resident of the ward. Goodbye Cardio-care and Geriatrics, hello C-3, with all of the fame and fortune that came with it. The Administrator, in fact, would often say in a giddy voice that C-3 stood for, "Comas, Cosmetic surgery, and Cash." And there was lots of cash.

In less than a year everything was standardized. Including the tummy tucks. After the medical coma was induced, the *clients* were pretty much on autopilot. They were all monitored by one central computer. It looked like something straight off the Starship Enterprise. It had been part of a generous grant from the Department of Defense. This was still a sore point for Jeff. He was the lone dissenter.

"What are you so worried about, Jeff?" the Administrator asked.

"They're from the Department of Defense, for crying out loud!" Jeff said.

"Yeah, and they are THE experts in bio-computer technology," a Senior Resident said.

"Ever wonder how they got that way? Or why our *diet* is so important to them?" Jeff asked.

"They told us, Dr. Combs," the Administrator said, "Sleep research for Deep Space missions."

"It makes sense if you think about it Jeff," the Senior Resident said, "It's a win-win situation. We get top notch equipment and they get a field of research subjects."

"We don't really know what that computer does," Jeff said.

"I'm sure it brainwashes them and turns them all into Republicans," the Administrator said sarcastically. Everyone except Jeff laughed.

"Doesn't it bother any of you how eager they were to *partner* with us?" Jeff asked.

"Oh yeah, their three-hundred-seventy-five million dollar grant bothered the hell out of me," the Administrator said. More laughter. "Dr. Combs, this is a wonderful thing for the hospital. Relax. Everything is going to be alright."

"I hope you're right," Jeff said. Turned out, he wasn't.

Jeff walked into the Nurse's Station. There was a bank of thirty-two monitors, one for each client, offering continuous displays of heart rate, breathing, and brain activity. Under each monitor was a steady print out of data. The Department of Defense system was across the hall in a secure windowless room. *What were they doing in there?* Jeff wondered.

When the system first went on line, Jeff was allowed to view a brief demonstration. The Tech stroked the top of the monitor, "How you doing Beauty?' he asked. He turned back to Jeff, "From Sleeping Beauty? Get it?"

What Jeff didn't get, was why a gazillion dollar computer was only displaying the same data as their simple monitors. "Do you track anything more than that?" Jeff asked.

"Sure. We monitor the…" A government agent interrupted him.

"Dr. Combs we are very concerned with the patient's health," the agent said.

"They're clients. And that's my department. This gizmo…" Jeff said.

"Beauty," the Tech interjected.

Jeff cleared his throat. "Beauty has got to be more than a glorified blood pressure monitor."

"Dr. Combs you've been briefed on our interest in your work here for Deep Space applications," the agent said. Jeff didn't trust them then, and now, a year later, he trusted them even less.

Jeff glanced down at the bank of monitors. Client number thirty-one's brain waves suddenly spiked. A one to two second spike was normal. This one held four full seconds. *That's odd,* Jeff thought. He grabbed the printout. There were random spikes throughout the last five hours, then, out of the blue, another four second spike. He flipped back through the printout. Five hours earlier he found another four second spike. The five hour pattern continued throughout the printout.

Jeff grabbed the next client's printout. It didn't take him long to find the same pattern, a four second spike every five hours. He glanced over at the secure room. *Something IS going on.* Jeff went through every printout. While none of the spikes occurred at the same time, still the pattern was consistent. Every client was the same, a four second spike every five hours. *Why hasn't anybody brought this to my attention?* Jeff thought. *Why would they?* he reasoned. *A four second spike is well below the threshold of concern. The five hour interval would insure that it only happened once on any given shift. Easy to see how they missed it.*

Jeff grabbed several printouts and headed for the Administrator's office. He couldn't help but notice how much the hospital had changed in the last year. Everything was new and fresh. He passed several life-size before and after posters of all their happy and successful dieters. *Dieters?* It still bothered him. He remembered interviewing one prospective client, a wealthy investment banker, who was willing to pay any price for the chance of getting thin.

"So your Coma Diet is gonna make me a new man, right Doc?"

"Well, it will make you a thinner man. No guarantees on being a new one," Jeff answered.

"Right, but, three or four months from now, all this extra lard I'm carrying around will be a thing of the past, right?"

"That's up to you," Jeff answered.

"What's that mean?" the man asked.

"You will be at least eighty pounds lighter when you leave this hospital. We can pretty much guarantee that. However, all the studies indicate that if you don't change your lifestyle, your body will do everything in its power to regain the weight," he said as he studied the man's reaction.

"I don't care about that Doc. If your diet works once, it'll work twice. Hell, I'll just check myself in here once a year if I need to."

The man's candid response troubled him. Jeff just couldn't comprehend how desperate you had to be to give up three of four months of your life to be thin. Especially on a yearly basis? That was insane.

Jeff stormed into the Administrator's office. "You've got to do something," Jeff said. He laid the printouts down and shared his discovery.

The Administrator looked up from the printouts. Even after hearing Jeff's concerns, he said, "This doesn't mean anything."

"It means they're doing something to our patients," Jeff said.

"Clients," the man corrected him.

"Whatever the hell we call them. They're still our responsibility," he said.

"Dr. Combs, how many clients have gone through the program so far?"

"Counting the current class, around one-hundred."

"One-hundred and three to be precise. And, have there been *ANY* complaints? Any clients dissatisfied with the results?"

"No. But…"

"But nothing Doctor. We're the groundbreakers on something phenomenal here." Jeff couldn't help but notice the Administrator's office. Corinthian leather and oak was everywhere. There were photos of him golfing with celebrities and politicians. There were several magazine covers with his smiling face on them. The Administrator stood up. "Dr. Combs, we are helping people realize lifelong dreams. We are changing lives. We are making a difference. And don't forget, our clients are very influential, very wealthy people."

"Yeah at three-hundred thousand a pop they better be."

"Dr. Combs, I don't need to lecture you about the high costs of medical care, do I? And, let's not forget that this was your idea, remember?" Somehow, Jeff didn't think that was entirely true.

"What would you like me to do, Dr. Combs? Kick out the government researchers? Tell the board we made a mistake? Too bad about all the renovations? And maybe we should just give back all the grant money?" he asked sarcastically.

"I'm just saying that they're hiding something. They're not telling us the whole truth about their little Deep Space project. The spikes prove it," Jeff said.

"They prove nothing. It's probably just their system running routine scans or something," the Administrator said.

"That's just it," he said. "We don't know what the spikes are all about. They don't share anything with us. I don't trust them."

"Maybe you're just too close to this," the Administrator said somberly.

"What's that supposed to mean?" he asked.

"Maybe you should back away a little. The system practically runs itself now. Besides, Leno's been bugging me to have you on. And everybody wants you to speak at their conference."

"Can we just ask them about the spikes?" Then he struck a nerve. "I mean, can you imagine the lawsuit if these spikes scrambled one of our *influential and wealthy* client's brain or something?" he asked. That question struck pay dirt.

The next day, Jeff was in the office of the government representative. The tech explained complicated algorithms and something he called 'pings'. He said those were responsible for the spikes. It was a harmless anomaly. It affected the monitoring system, not the clients. It made sense. That's what bothered him. It was too convenient.

The following day, Dr. Jeff Combs was on the Tonight Show. Within a week he was speaking at Princeton. Throw in a book tour and six weeks flew by. He felt energized. It was nice to have the rich and famous pandering to him. Maybe he was too paranoid. Maybe the Administrator was right. The numbers clearly supported their work. They were hailed as saviors by the morbidly obese—those that could afford their services anyway.

The first day back at the hospital was exciting. Work was beginning on a new wing. Within a few months they would be able to handle up to a hundred clients at a time. This was becoming big business. Even better— the government provided the equipment, underwrote the building, and provided an additional hundred thousand per client they were allowed to *monitor*. Life was good.

Jeff stood in front of the monitors and scanned the fairly boring readouts. He picked up the printouts. The spikes were still there, like the tech said they would be. Something was different though. "Dear God!" Jeff said. The spikes were getting worse. They were up to fifteen seconds every two hours. Jeff rushed across the hall. He started banging on the window. "Open up! Let me in! NOW!"

An armed guard jerked the door open. "Can I help you, Dr. Combs?"

"Yeah, you can get whoever's back there stroking Beauty to tell me what the hell is going on!"

He attempted to side-step the guard. "Sir, I can't let you in there."

The door to the inner office opened. It was the Tech. "It's alright. He can come in."

Jeff walked thru and the Tech shut the door. He was pacing back and forth, running his fingers through his hair. "A sleep study. It's just supposed to be a sleep study. Monitor REM and brain activity. Deep Space Project. Spooky stuff. That's all. Not this. Not this."

"What are you talking about?" Jeff asked.

"They changed the data. Changed the spikes. They're pumping it in there like crazy now."

"Pumping what? What the hell are you talking about?"

The Tech continued to pace. "Beauty is mine! I designed her. I built her. And they're jacking with her."

"What is Beauty supposed to do? And don't give me that BS about algorithms and pings."

The Tech laughed, "Pretty lame, huh?"

Jeff stared at him, angry and curious, waiting for an explanation.

"Beauty can read minds."

"Read minds?"

"Well, sorta. Actually she can see what you're dreaming. She can record your dreams. Play them back for some Psych-Doc to interpret. That sort of stuff," he said.

"I didn't think we had technology like that," Jeff said in more of an asking tone.

The Tech laughed, "We don't. I do."

"Why is the government so interested in our program?" he asked.

"Are you kidding? This is a gold mine here."

Jeff's puzzled look encouraged him to explain.

"OK, normal setting, I hook Beauty up to one guy and get maybe six hours of dream data out of a twenty-four hour period."

"Here", the Tech continued, "I get continuous feed, twenty-four/seven, from thirty-two people at one time. The data is immense. We had to upgrade the crap out of Beauty just to handle it."

"What do you do with the data?"

"Huh?"

"The dreams. What do you do with them?"

"You're missing the point. They don't care about the dreams."

"What then?"

"Input. They never told me about the input. It's not fair to Beauty. That's not what she does."

Input? The spikes. The intervals. What were they up to?

The Tech stopped pacing and began stroking the monitor, "Girl, you know it wasn't my idea." He looked back at Jeff, "I had no way of knowing what it would do to her. How she would handle it."

"What input?" Jeff asked.

Just then the door burst open. "I'll take it from here," the agent said to the Tech. The glare in his eyes was obvious. "Dr. Combs, if you would come with me, please." Jeff didn't fail to notice the guard's hand resting on his pistol.

"What are you people doing to my patients?"

"In due time, Doctor," the agent answered. He added, "And they're clients, remember, not patients."

Jeff followed the agent and the guard, "Where are we going?" he asked.

"Somewhere safe," the man answered. Jeff found himself in an unmarked office in the basement of the hospital. The security was ridiculous: armed guards at the first two doors they went through; pass card with a thumb print scan at the last one.

"You've got to be kidding me," Jeff said.

"We're very serious about our work, Dr. Combs," the agent answered.

35

Jeff stepped through the door. The room was abuzz with activity. Monitors and high tech computers everywhere. The agent gave Jeff some time to soak it all in. There were thirty-two stations. Each one consisted of three monitors. The top one showed the client asleep. The middle one was a replica of the monitor in the nurse's station. The bottom one was beyond belief. Colors and images rolled across the screen. In one, a man was fishing while watering a garden. In another, a lady was dancing with Elvis. Each monitor apparently displaying the dreams of that client. Some were nonsensical, some erotic, some just a bizarre montage of images and sounds.

Jeff turned to ask a question. The agent put his finger to his lip. "Just watch," he said, and pointed at client number twenty-six's dream monitor. Jeff was stunned as it changed from a man running through a dark forest to CNN. Wolf Blitzer was reporting on immigration issues.

"What the hell?" Jeff asked.

The agent pointed to a small office, "Shall we?" He closed the door as they went in and sat down. "I don't know how much our overly anxious creator told you about our little problem," he said. Jeff played enough poker to know that the agent was looking for a 'tell'. Those two words "creator" and "problem" were bouncing around inside his head.

Jeff played his hand, "Enough for me to want some answers." He leaned forward and waited.

The agent blinked first. "As you know the Deep Space Project…"

Jeff cut him off, "Stop! Just stop. We are way beyond that. We both know this has nothing to do with any Deep Space Project."

"That's where you're wrong, Dr. Combs." Jeff leaned back. It was his turn to look for a tell. He motioned with his hands for the man to keep talking. "Imagine a Deep Space flight that takes fifteen to twenty years to reach its target. I mean destination."

Jeff nodded, *Creator, problem, target—got it.*

"Twenty years there and twenty years back and our thirty-five year old astronaut is seventy-five years old. That's where hyper-sleep comes in."

"Hyper-sleep?"

"Suspended animation. We theorize we can slow the aging process down from forty years to less than five; eight at the most."

Jeff processed this as the agent continued. "Your Coma Diet was a godsend. It accelerated our research a thousand percent."

"So I hear."

The agent studied Jeff before continuing. "Even if we can slow the aging process, and all evidence suggests that we can, we still have a huge problem."

"Which is?"

"Knowledge, Dr. Combs."

"I'm not following you."

The agent seemed to relax. "Imagine if you were *out of the loop* for forty years. You have no idea what's happened in your absence. You don't know who the president is or who won any of the last forty World Series. You know nothing of popular culture, movies, and fashion; much less the state of world affairs. You would be returning to a very different, maybe even dangerous, world. The last forty years are a blank to you."

"As though you were in a coma," Jeff said.

"Precisely, Dr. Combs."

Jeff connected the dots. *The spikes!* "You're pumping the news into them."

"We're keeping them informed."

"Forty years of hearing what's wrong with Planet Earth and they may not want to come back."

"Maybe so, but when they wake up they'll have a full memory of everything they missed."

Jeff sat back. He studied the agent. The story made sense. In fact it was genius. Still, something didn't add up. He decided to call the bluff. "That's all well and good, but what about our *little problem*?"

The man chewed on his lower lip. He stood up and closed the blinds. He sat back down and stared across the desk. Jeff didn't flinch. The agent said, "Beauty has developed something of a bug, a programming glitch in her system."

"That's not how her *creator* describes it," Jeff lied.

"He's eccentric. He wants to believe this thing has acquired intelligence, a higher level of conscience. He thinks it picked up traces of humanity during the pings of information uploading."

"Beauty has a conscience?"

"Hardly. The thing's a flipping computer. That's it. Nothing more. It processes data, analyzes solutions, and solves problems. That's it. One plus one has to equal two."

"And when it doesn't?" Jeff asked. The agent just stared at him. Jeff took a gamble. "It creates a program to fix the problem doesn't it?"

The man looked beaten. "It's just a machine. It lacks logic and common sense. It only sees life as ones and zeroes. If something seems out of balance it will work to fix it."

Jeff processed what he was hearing. "The news," he said.

The man shook his head. "Beauty doesn't understand hyperbole, or political rhetoric. She interprets what she receives as a sort of mathematical formula. A problem for her to solve."

"So if she receives a steady diet of cable news, she must consider the world to be a very dangerous place," he said.

"You could say that," he responded. The man was clearly anxious about something.

"I'm not entirely sure I fully understand the problem," Jeff said. "I mean, while I don't particularly like it, isn't Beauty nothing more than a glorified VCR? Or, at worst, a TV for your dreams?" he asked.

"I wish that's all she was now," the man said.

"Now?" Jeff asked.

The man clenched his teeth and drew in a deep breath. He let out a long sigh. "Look, I don't for a second think that Beauty has somehow become sentient. Hell, maybe it would be better if she did. I don't know," he said. He stared off into the distance for a moment.

Why is he suddenly being so open? Jeff wondered. *Something happened and it's scaring the hell out of him.*

"There's no denying the fact that Beauty is different now," he said. "It's nothing we can see in her programming. All that seems the same."

Jeff noted that he drug out the word "seems." "But it's not," he interjected.

"No, it's not. I didn't want to believe it," he said as he shook his head. "But it seems irrefutable at this point."

Jeff decided it was time to be direct. "Okay, I have two questions. First, why are you suddenly sharing all of this with me?" he eyed the man, looking for any significant responses. "And second, what has got you so worried?"

The man chuckled. "Obvious, huh?"

Jeff gave him a nod and a smirk that, combined, implied, "Duh."

The man stood and walked a small loop in his office. "Okay, full disclosure," he said as he gave Jeff a thumbs up gesture. "I was actually coming to talk with you today. And then you showed up banging on the door."

"You increased the 'spikes'," he said. "It got my attention."

"Yeah, well, that wasn't us," the man said rather flatly.

"What are you saying?" Jeff asked.

"I'm saying that Beauty did it. She increased the spikes," he said.

"Wait a minute," Jeff said as he considered what the man was saying. "On her own? Her decision?" he asked.

"Apparently, the man," said. "We were content with the data we were receiving from the single short burst spikes of news programing once every five hours."

"Why did she increase it?" Jeff asked and then added, "And with what?"

"We don't know why," he answered. "At first we thought it was a programming glitch. We've been assured that didn't happen." He continued walking and then suddenly stopped. "I can tell you what some of the increased pings are. Not all of them, but some of them."

"Why not all of them?" Jeff asked.

"We honestly don't know what some of them are," he said. "It appears to be some random electronic bursts that she's sending."

"That's weird," Jeff said. "What about the ones you know. What are they?"

The man laughed, "You're gonna think I'm pulling your chain, but it's the God's honest truth." He stared at Jeff for a few seconds before continuing. "Cooking shows," he said. "She's sending them cooking shows," he said with an amused look on his face.

"Seriously?" Jeff asked.

"Seriously," he answered. "She's sending them things like 'Iron Chef' and 'Cupcake Wars'." Jeff took in the new and very strange information. "Her crazy creator says that Beauty made a choice to do it. An intelligent choice," the man emphasized.

He stopped walking and faced Jeff. "I don't buy it," he said. "I think it's still technically within the parameters of her programming."

"How so?" Jeff asked.

"Problem solving," the man said. "She sees, or thinks she sees, a problem and she creates a solution to it."

"So what 'problem' does Beauty think she sees?" Jeff asked.

"We're still working on that," the man said. "The theories I'm hearing are not good ones."

"Can you elaborate?" Jeff asked. He was starting to get on edge about this whole conversation.

"Maybe a little," the man said. "Beauty seems to understand, on some level, that the people she's hooked up to are obese."

That's kinda obvious, Jeff thought.

"And, that they are being forced to lose weight," he said. "At least, that's what we surmise." He continued, "She also seems to understand

41

that the nature of the world, based on the newsfeeds, is in turmoil. Things are out of order."

The man scratched his head and then rubbed his chin as he gathered his thoughts. "Dr. Combs, have you followed up on your clients?" he asked.

"Of course," he said. "They typically get a clean bill of health thirty days after the program. That's usually the last we see them."

The man looked deep into Jeff's eyes. "It might interest you to know, Dr. Combs, that of the seventy-one clients that completed your *diet*," he said, making the obligatory quotation mark signs with his fingers, "exactly one-hundred percent of them bought very large shares of stock within sixty days of leaving the hospital."

"Our clients are very wealthy. That shouldn't be so surprising," he said.

"Maybe not," the man said. "But, what are the odds they would all buy the same two stocks? So much of it, that as a group, they are now the controlling interests."

It was Jeff's turn to bite his lower lip. He didn't like this. "What stocks did they buy?"

"Quadricon, for one," the man answered.

Jeff knew that name from somewhere, but couldn't quite place it. Alarms went off in head when the man spelled it out for him. "Quadricon is the primary weapons contractor for our military's satellite defense systems."

"Oh my God!" Jeff said. "What the hell?"

"Exactly," the man said. "It's why we needed to talk."

They both stared at each other in stunned silence. *I understand why he's so anxious*, Jeff thought. "I hate to ask," Jeff said, "But what's the other one?"

The man shook his head as he answered, "Krispy Kreme Donuts."

-3-

-Face to Face-

"For now we see through a glass, darkly, but then
face to face. Now I know in part;
but then shall I know,
even as also I am known."
St. Paul, I Corinthians 13:12

S al rested his hand against the door. He knew he should go in. He had to go in. This time was different, he told himself. This time was...he paused, *What if it doesn't work? What then?* He waited. Hoping for an answer—a sign, something to assure him that he was doing the right thing. A sharp beeping sound erupted behind him. He turned to see the Head Nurse at her desk. She smiled and nodded her head as if to say, "Go ahead Sal. It's where you're needed". At least that was how he interpreted her casual nod.

"It always starts this way, doesn't it?" he said out loud. He took a deep breath and pressed against the aluminum handle. He stepped into a room that was both familiar and completely unrelated to any other part of his life. He scanned the machines, the flowing curtains, the cursory flowers that lined the window sill. Once again, Salvatore Vincent Scarlatti, Sal to everyone who knew him, entered a world that he had no business being in. A world that was as foreign to his everyday life as a carpenter as...well...as this one was. It was a modern-day hospital room, a critical-care unit in fact. There were machines and devices crowding the room. Sal had absolutely no idea what most of them were for. This was a strange place, a solemn place. A place where technology and science rubbed against the harsh realities of the human experience. Sometimes, not often enough though, technology won the day. More often than not,

45

however, mortality, as it had done for countless eons, won the endless battle. No matter how many machines they hooked you up to, or how long they could extend your body's ability to breathe in and breathe out—in the end, everyone loses the battle.

He let the door close softly behind him, holding his hand against it to prevent that loud clicking noise that he knew would come. He hated that noise. The way it would broadcast his presence to everyone within earshot. Sal preferred to remain unnoticed. Nobody needed to see what he was about to do.

He turned back around for a quick glance and to steady his nerves. He was exceptionally nervous. That didn't happen too much anymore. He saw that several of the nurses had gathered for a quick conference with the Head Nurse. He saw through their charade. The only reason they were huddled together was because he was here. All eyes were on him. He could see it written across their faces. They were rarely wrong. Their timing was almost always perfect. They knew why he was here. Hell, they had called him. It was their idea.

Sal gazed down at the motionless figure on the bed before him. The old man looked so frail. He could practically count his ribs through the thin hospital sheet. He told himself, over and over again, that tonight wouldn't be any different. He had been here dozens and dozens of times before. It was almost becoming routine. Almost. The second he glanced into the darkened and withered face, he knew he was wrong. Tonight was different—very different.

Nearly all of the people he had "helped" over the years were total strangers to him. Not tonight. This would be the first time that someone knew, in advance, exactly what his presence meant. He had no idea how the man would react. Would he be shocked? Afraid? Amused? Or have Security throw him out? *Knowing him, he'll probably just laugh,* Sal thought and then added, *until it's over.* By then, he would understand. There would be no room for doubt or confusion.

He glanced back down at the man. The monitor on the wall, the only one he halfway understood, was the only real indicator that he was still alive. His breathing had nearly ceased. The color was rapidly draining from his face. *With or without me,* Sal thought, *this is going to happen. May as well be with me.* He stepped forward. Tears formed in the corners of his eyes. He hoped that this day would never come. He knew, however, that it always did. Death eventually came for everyone. As he stared at the man, he was filled with a deep sense of compassion and love. *This is good,* he thought. *This is right.*

He gently placed a hand on the man's shoulder. He let it rest there for a moment, feeling the slight movement of his breathing. He sighed and lightly shook him.

The man opened his eyes with a startled gasp. His reaction was that of a man who had been summoned from a faraway place. He seemed confused. He could read the "what am I doing here?" expression on his face. Sal smiled down at him. He felt such love for the man. "Hello Father," he said.

The old man strained his eyes to see. He seemed to be looking through a fog. His confusion slowly changed to understanding. "You?" the old man asked. "What are you doing here?" He strained to look around the room. They were alone. A slight chuckle escaped his lips as realization dawned on him. He knew what this was about. Of course he did. "Sal," the old man struggled to speak, "please, this is nonsense. You don't belong here. Go home."

His words struck a chord with Sal. He had been dreading this moment for years now. "You're right," he said, as he lightly squeezed the old man's shoulder, "I don't belong here. I'm just a carpenter," he said. "And not a very good one at that," he added with a smile.

Salvatore Vincent Scarlatti, a Journeyman with the 583rd Local, was a man who, for the last seven years, built sets for off-Broadway productions. He didn't mind the work. It gave him a sense that he was creating something. That he was a part of something bigger than himself. He shook his head. The old man was right. He had absolutely no business, whatsoever, being here. He really wasn't qualified to do what he was about to do. It went against everything in his nature. He was a "behind the scenes" kind of guy. He steered clear of the limelight. Perhaps that's why building sets seemed perfectly suited to him. Still, there was no escaping it, like it or not, he had a job to do. A job he never asked for and sure as hell didn't want. But, as the guys he worked with would say as they shrugged their shoulders, "What-cha gonna do?" He smiled and slid his hand down to the old man's hand. Their fingers intertwined.

"Sal, Sal, Sal," the old man whispered.

"I know," Sal said, "What-cha gonna do?"

Sal stared into the old man's eyes. He remembered the first time they had met—what was it, five? Six years ago? The words of Sal's grandmother rang in his ears, "You want to know about the spirit world? Forget the Pentecostals, they ain't got a clue. If you wanna know about the spirit world you go find you a priest Sallie, you gotta find a priest." And that's exactly what he did.

Father Dominique Petri listened with a detached sense of interest in Sal's story. Sal couldn't tell from the old priest's expression what sort of impact his story was having. *This guy would make a hell of a poker player*, Sal thought, *no way to read him.* As soon as Sal finished, he said, "So that's it, Father." He looked at the priest who was sitting with his head resting calmly on his clasped hands as though he were in deep thought. After several moments of awkward silence, Sal finally spoke up, "So, Father, what do you think?"

"Salvatore, is it?" the priest asked.

"Call me Sal," he answered.

"Yes, Sal," the priest responded. "The real question, Sal," he said, "is what do you think?"

"What do I think?" Sal asked. "What the hell do I know….uh, sorry, Father."

"No need for apologies, Sal."

Sal cleared his throat. "I mean, I'm just a carpenter. I don't know what to think about this. It's not really my field," Sal said and continued, "I was hoping you could help me figure it out."

"You must have some idea about what it means," the priest countered.

"Other than the obvious," Sal said.

"Which is?" the priest asked.

"Well, that I've lost my freaking mind," Sal answered.

"Is that what you think?"

"No," Sal shook his head, "not really."

"Then what?" the priest asked.

"Well, it's this whole death thing. I mean, why me? I'm a nobody carpenter. I don't know about this stuff." Sal was deep in thought. He was waiting for the priest to say something—anything. Finally he said, "The first time, OK maybe I thought I'm losing it, but after the second and the third time, well it's kinda hard to make this stuff up."

"Tell me about that first time, Sal," the old priest said.

Sal didn't want to go there. It was a painful memory. He grimaced and said, "You really want to hear it?"

The priest leaned forward, resting his elbows on his legs, "Yes, Sal, I really do want to hear it."

Sal swallowed. "Alright," he said. He took a deep breath and tried to calm his beating heart. "Here goes," he said. Already his mind was filling with images from that fateful night; images that continued to haunt his dreams. He began, "It was raining—really coming down." Sal paused, wondering if he should mention how much the rain frightened him to this day. He shook his head "No" to the conversation going on inside, and continued, "Me and this kid, Tally, we was waiting for the bus up on 95th street. We had just put a long day in fixing these door jambs on a high rise. The other guys wanted us to catch a few brews with 'em before heading home—but me and Tally was ready to call it quits. I was ready to get home and Tally said he had a paper to do or something. I think he was taking some business class at the community college." He was lost in reflection for a few moments. Finally he continued, "He was a good kid. Real sharp." He shook his head again and bit his lower lip as the memories came flooding back over him.

The priest noticed the gesture and seemed to understand the difficulty that Sal was experiencing. "Then what happened?" he asked.

"So, me and Tally was standing under that little bus shelter with our tool bags, trying not to get drenched." The story seemed to be playing out again in Sal's mind. "Tally says, 'What the hell is that?' Sal started to apologize again and decided against it. "There's this car flying around the corner like a bat out of….well, you know, he was driving crazy, coming fast," Sal said. "I can tell that the car's gonna hit us. I see the driver's eyes—like he's high on crack or drunk on his ass." He looked at the priest, wondering if he crossed the line again. The old priest just nodded for him to continue. "So I reach for the kid, like I know he's gonna get the worst of it. I grab him, trying to pull him out of the way—but it's no use. I'm too late. The car's moving too fast. That guy plows right into Tally. Kid never had a chance," he said.

The old priest took note of the tears forming in Sal's eyes. His years of counseling taught him to just sit silently and wait. This was Sal's story. He would tell it at his pace. A younger version of himself would have pushed for a conclusion. The sooner the story was over, the sooner he could dispense words of wisdom. He smiled inwardly at his young naïve self. If there was one thing he learned in his many years of shepherding the Lord's flock, it was just how little he actually knew. He came out of seminary thinking that people were coming to him to get the answers to life's questions. He learned, however, over the years, they were mostly coming just to talk. They didn't need answers near as much as they just needed someone to listen to them. He was surprised to learn that letting someone share their pain, in a nonjudgmental and sympathetic setting, was therapeutic in and of itself. It was humbling to admit, but it was true: his silence helped many more people than his talking ever did.

He let Sal take a moment to gather his thoughts. When he was ready, he continued, "The force of the hit drives Tally into me and smashes us both into the back of that little bus shelter." All color drained from Sal's face as he re-entered that moment. "I can feel the front of that car. It just sorta ripped right through Tally and is pressing up against my chest. He took the full impact of the hit." Sal stood to his feet. In his mind the car had materialized in the priest's office. "I pried myself out from behind Tally and he just flopped over the hood. That bastard in the car," he said, and this time added, "Sorry Father."

"It's alright, Sal," the priest said, "then what happened?"

"That bastard...uh, the driver, he jerked open the door and started running down the street laughing his head off." The fury of the moment overwhelmed Sal. The anger was raw and fresh. He gritted his teeth. "I stepped around and grabbed Tally's hand."

"The kid was ripped in two. Blood was everywhere. It pooled out of his mouth when he tried to speak." Tears were streaming down Sal's face as he relived that night. "I told him to hold on, an ambulance is coming." He looked at the priest as if to explain, "I was hoping one was coming anyway." Sal continued, "Tally said something about a business paper being due....and that's it. That's all he got out before he...before he died." Sal stopped talking, the priest knew, however, the story was far from over.

After a few moments, he gently prodded Sal with a question, "So he died while you were holding his hand?"

"Yeah," Sal muttered.

"And?" the priest asked.

51

"And then," Sal said, "IT happened."

The priest waited. He knew that Sal would fill in the silence when he was ready.

"So he died while I'm holding his hand, and then everything just goes black."

"For Tally?" the priest asked.

"No. Well, yeah. But not just Tally. It goes black for both of us," Sal said. Then he corrected himself, "Well, not totally black." He struggled to describe what he experienced. "There were these lights and shapes—like tiny stars or swirling fireworks. They kept getting closer and closer. I completely forgot about Tally until he stepped beside me."

"We just stood there staring at each other for a few seconds, trying to make some sense out of what we were seeing. Tally was the first one to speak." Sal sat back down.

"What did he say?" the priest asked.

"He asked me if we were dead," Sal said. Before the priest could respond, Sal said, "I was thinking, you are Tally—but then I began to wonder if maybe I was too. I mean, what else could it be?" Sal considered his own question for a moment before continuing. "Then Tally gets this look on his face, like he suddenly understands, like everything is perfect in the universe and he's happy as a clam. He puts his hand on my shoulder, smiles at me and says, 'Take care of yourself Sal', and then he just...." Sal paused.

"Just what?" the priest asked.

Sal wrinkled his face in pure consternation. "He just disintegrated...no that's not it," he said. "It was like one of those Star Trek shows where somebody gets transported. He sort of shimmered into these tiny particles that started swirling in a circle—you know, like something going down a drain. And then, all of those tiny pieces just shot out into the darkness. Each piece flew towards those lights or stars, or whatever they were, and disappeared right into the center of them."

Sal looked up at the priest. "I was thinking the same thing was probably going to happen to me next—and I was getting kinda panicky, looking around, wondering when it was gonna happen—and the darkness, the lights, it all just disappeared. By the time I realized it was gone I was back beside Tally's body, draped across that hood, and I was still holding his hand."

Sal sat stone-faced before the priest. He had nothing else to say. The priest spoke up after a few moments, "Sal, I'm sure you understand that you were in a traumatic situation. Our minds can play amazing tricks on us..."

Sal interrupted him, "I know. I know. I thought the same thing. I thought it was all in my head. None of it really happened. Hell, how could it?" Sal cracked his knuckles. "Till it happened again," Sal said.

"There was another accident?" the priest asked.

"No," Sal said. "The second time was different. It was my dad. I was at the nursing home when he died."

"Did you have a similar..." the priest searched for the right word, "uh, experience this time as well?"

"Yes and no," Sal said. "Same as before, he died while I was holding his hand and just like before everything went black except for those swirling stars and lights."

The priest leaned back in his chair, suddenly very interested in hearing Sal's story. "It was pretty freaky, one second I'm holding my dying dad's hand and the next second I'm sorta floating beside him in outer space."

"Outer space?" Father Petri asked. Remembering Sal's Star Trek reference, he asked, "So you believe you were transported into space?"

53

"Not literally," Sal answered. "I mean my body never left my dad's side. It all happened in the blink of an eye—it's like time doesn't matter out there."

"You said this time was different," the priest said, hoping to keep Sal on track.

"Yeah, I was standing or floating out there with my dad and I saw that same expression come over his face that came over Tally's. And what was really odd," Sal started to say.

The priest thought to himself, *Odder than what you've said so far?* He just smiled and nodded for Sal to continue.

"I looked out into those stars and it was like I could feel Tally looking back at me—like he was out there waiting. And I was thinking that was good because my dad would really like Tally. My dad seemed to sense what's about to happen because he looked at me and said 'I ain't ready to leave you Sallie—not just yet.' So, I reached out to him just as he started that shimmering thing, you know, like Tally did. I can still see him smiling as it's happening. He turns into those glowing particles and they all start swirling in a spiral, just like Tally." The priest nodded his head.

"So I looked off to the distance and my dad's...what would you call it? His atoms? Or maybe his essence? Hell I don't know. Not exactly something they teach you in carpentry school," Sal forced a chuckle. The priest rolled his fingers in the air as if to say, "Continue".

"Right," Sal said, "So my dad's spirit, I guess that's what it was, it started spiraling towards those lights—shooting straight towards them like Tally did. And then, all of a sudden, he just looped back in a giant U-turn and come barreling straight back at me!" Sal said. "It kind of startled me and I tried to jump back, but there ain't nothing behind me but more open space. I raised my hands up and started to scream cause it's gonna hit me right in the face, and there ain't nothing I can do about it." The panic on Sal's face was evident.

The priest pondered the psychological implications of Sal's story. He wondered what it might say about Sal's relationship with his Dad; or the obvious unresolved grief he still had over Tally. He made mental notes of some of the key points of Sal's story. Perhaps they would go back to them later. "So your Dad's spirit came back to you?" he asked.

"Yeah, but more than that. It hit me full on in the face. It was like you threw a bucket of cold water on me. I mean, I felt it punch through me. I felt it work itself into me. At first I was in full-on panic mode—not sure what was happening; but after a minute or so, I relaxed." He looked into the old priest's face before continuing. "It sorta comes to me what just happened. And when it does, there's this weird feeling that just bounces inside of me—and I understand, more than that, I KNOW. I mean I really know what happened. And it's pretty freaking amazing."

The priest waited a moment. He was slightly irritated at being goaded, still he played along, "OK, Exactly what is it that you think you KNOW Sal?" he asked.

"It's my Dad's essence, his spirit. It entered me," Sal said, with a touch of both pride and reverence.

Maybe that's what this is all about, the priest thought. "Sal," he said, in a comforting tone, "It's not uncommon for people to have a sense that their loved ones live on through them."

"No, that's not it," Sal objected, maybe a little too harshly. "He came INTO me…he made a decision and he chose to continue in me instead of doing what Tally did."

The priest gave him a quizzical look, "So what exactly are you saying?" the priest asked.

"Well," Sal said, "this sort of thing happened enough times now that I have come up with what you might call a *hypothesis*." He said the word slowly to make sure he pronounced it right.

"And what is your hypothesis?" the priest asked.

"I figure it's like this," Sal said. "When you die your spirit, your essence, whatever you wanna call it, returns to the universe, and somehow, you become a part of the universe. I ain't got that all worked out yet. I never really studied on it. But, I think you're given a choice. Right at the last second, you can choose to join the universe—become one with it, like Tally did. Or you can send your essence back into your loved ones and wait to join the universe later on; like after they die, or something like that." Sal eyed the priest, wondering what he thought of all this.

"What would lead you to that conclusion?" the priest asked.

"Well," Sal said, "A couple of times, I was with someone when they died and these other folks just showed up."

The priest considered what Sal was saying. "It's a common hope," the priest said, "that our loved ones will meet us on the other side."

"I know that," Sal said, "but this was different. It was like they had been with the person the whole time."

Father Petri studied Sal. He ran back through his mental notes of key points. He compared them with his limited psychological training. He tried to connect the dots of Sal's psyche. Was it driven by grief? Issues with his dad? Narcissism? A messiah complex? Dear God, he hoped it wasn't going to be another one of those. He finally spoke up, "How many times has this happened to you now, Sal?"

Sal thought. He ran through some mental calculations. It really was hard to remember them all. "Let's see, it's been seven years since Tally died; and it was about three months after that my dad died...that's really when it started."

"When what started?" the priest asked.

"Well, when I did some testing to see if what was happening was real or not." Sal said.

"Now you've really got me curious," the old priest said. "Exactly how did you conduct these *tests*?" He emphasized the word.

The look in the priest's eye unnerved Sal. "Nothing crazy or illegal," Sal said, rather defensively. "Well maybe crazy," he smiled. "I kept visiting the nursing home, making on like I wanted to keep in touch with my dad's friends, that sort of stuff. But, what I was really doing was trying to find out which patients were the closest to death. The nurses all thought it was sweet that I was trying to work out my grief and maybe trying to make things right with my father—some sort of psycho-bullshit...uh, sorry Father, some sort of pyscho-babble. Anyway, I went along with it because they started pointing me towards the ones that were close to checking out. I cried and asked the nurses to call me when it was close. I wanted to be there to say good-bye." Sal smiled. "Of course they bought it, they all thought I needed closure or something," he chuckled.

They may have been right, the priest thought.

"Anyhow, I was there with about a half-dozen lonely old men when they breathed their last breath. I held their hand as they died," Sal said. "And without fail," he emphasized, "without fail. It happened the same way with every single one of them."

"Regardless of their faith?" the priest asked.

"Father," Sal said, "no offense, but I have no earthly idea what any of those men believed in—or didn't believe in, for that matter. No real idea how they lived their lives or what sort of a person they were. Most of them were unconscious when I met them for the first time. We didn't get to talk too much." He smiled.

"So," the priest said, "You're saying that whether they were a Christian or an Atheist, whether they lived a good life or were a miserable S.O.B.—they all had the exact same experience when they died?"

"That's how it happened," Sal said.

"I take it that these experiences didn't stop at that nursing home?" the priest asked.

"Hardly," Sal answered. "After I had proof that it wasn't just in my head, I started to wonder if maybe this wasn't a gift or something. So I started making friends at the ICU's and the Emergency Rooms around town."

"A gift?" the priest asked. *Dear* Lord, he thought, *here we go*. His question made Sal feel foolish for even mentioning it.

"Not like I'm a prophet or somebody special, because I'm not," Sal said with a worried look on his face. He searched for the right words. "It's just that I can sorta help folks make that transition. You know, from this life to the next, that's all." Then he added as an afterthought, "It ain't much. In fact, I think they'd probably be fine without me—but what am I supposed to do with this? Ignore it? Believe me, I tried." Sal said.

"So you visited places where you figured people were about to die so you could help them cross over?" the priest asked.

"Well, when you put it like that it makes me sound sorta creepy, doesn't it?" Sal asked.

"Does it?" the priest asked, with one raised eyebrow.

"Listen, Father, all I know is that it happened. Every single time. Jew or Baptist, drug addict or somebody's saintly mother—every single time, for every single person, it happened the same way."

The priest observed Sal for a moment. Maybe it was time to probe his level of faith. "What does all of this say to you about heaven, Sal?" the priest asked. Before he could answer, he continued, "About God? Where is God in these *visions* of yours?" He emphasized the word 'vision' in a way that reeked of sarcasm.

"Look," Sal said, "You're the priest. I'm just a stinking carpenter. What happened, happened. That's all I know. And I don't know anything about heaven or God. Never really saw either of them." He looked down at his hands and then back up at the priest. "Always the same—just the universe—that's it." Then Sal said, as though he just had an epiphany, "Hey, maybe the universe *is* God. Maybe that's all there is." He waited for the priest's response.

A soft smile broke out across the priest's face. "You do realize that's blasphemy, don't you Sal?" the priest asked.

Sal paused to gather his thoughts. "Father, I don't mean any offense. I really don't. I'm just trying to make sense out of all of this—that's all. And I'll be the first guy to say that I don't know shit from shinola.....sorry Father," he said. "I was just hoping you could help me."

The old priest smiled, "OK Sal," he said. "I don't have any answers for you." He reached out and patted Sal's knee. "But I'll make a promise to you, if you'd like."

"What's that?" Sal asked.

"We'll figure it out together," he said.

That was the beginning of a relationship that would cover five years of similar stories. Father Petri became Sal's confidant. Sal became his guilty pleasure. He never truly believed Sal's stories. He attributed them to a fruitful imagination and a troubled soul. He did, however, thoroughly enjoy hearing them. He continued, over the years, to use church teaching and theology to slowly bring Sal back into the fold. He believed that once Sal worked through his grief he would come to realize the folly of what he was saying. How could it be otherwise? After one particularly animated conversation where Sal was sharing his latest experience as death's personal usher, Father Petri asked, "Sal, you do realize that IF what you are saying is real—that it flies in the face of thousands of years of religious tradition? Christian, Jewish, Muslim—all of them are wrong if you're right."

"I've thought about that Father," Sal said. "I'm the last person to tell anybody, Buddhist or Baptist, that they're wrong. That they completely missed the mark on this whole God and eternity thing."

"I believe you, Sal," he said. "But that's exactly what you're saying," the priest countered. "You're saying the scriptures and teachings of the church are wrong. It's all one giant mistake."

"Maybe not," Sal objected.

"OK, then what ARE you saying?" he asked.

"I've been thinking on this for years," Sal said. "What if it's like this; what if I decided to write about what it would be like to take a trip to Fiji? Or Hawaii? Now, keep in mind, I ain't never been to either one of them. But I bet I could imagine what life would be like there. Wouldn't you figure? I could write about it just using my imagination. But, IF I ever actually went to Fiji, then I'd get the real picture of what it's like there." He paused and then asked, "You know what I mean?"

"Yes, Sal, I think I do," he said. "You're saying the writers of scripture wrote about how they imagined God and heaven and to be—but you've actually been there. So, what they could only imagine—well, you've actually seen." Even as he was answering Sal, the priest was remembering what the Apostle Paul wrote about his own attempt to explain his experiences with God. He could hear Paul's words echoing around in his mind, *"Now all we can see of God is like a cloudy picture in a mirror. Later we will see him face to face. We don't know everything, but then we will"*.

He couldn't help himself, "You're saying that your understanding changes when you come face to face with God."

"Yeah, I guess I am," Sal said.

The old priest looked up at Sal from his hospital bed. *I guess he thinks it's my turn now*, he thought. He struggled to get comfortable. It hurt to move. It hurt to lay still. It just hurt. Sal fluffed his pillow and the old man settled his head against it. He folded his hands across his chest. There was a flicker of amusement in his eyes. "Did the nurses call you?" he asked.

"Yeah. They said I should hurry," Sal said in a whisper.

"You just missed the Bishop," Father Petri said. "He gave me my Last Rites." He tried to moisten his lips and found that he lacked the strength or the spit to do so. Sal cradled his head and held a cup of water for him. Even with a straw, the water dribbled from his mouth. Sal dabbed his face with a napkin. "Thank you," the old priest said as Sal laid his head back against the pillow. His eyes fluttered several times as though he were falling back into a deep trance. Sal sat by his side— waiting. With his eyes closed, Father Petri asked, "So how's this work Sal?"

"Mostly," Sal said, "we just wait."

He cast his eyes towards the nurse's station, "They ever get it wrong?"

"Sometimes," Sal said and then added, "but not too often."

"No more mysteries after tonight Sal," the priest said, "no more crazy stories."

Sal smiled and nodded his head. He was going to miss Father Petri very much.

Remembering that much earlier conversation the priest said, with his remaining strength, "Face to face."

"Face to face," Sal agreed.

The old priest was smiling. He gasped for air. A confused look came across his face. Sal watched as clouds filled the old man's eyes. He was struggling to sit up. Something had gotten his attention. He could hear the hope and the love etched into the single word that the old man asked out loud, "Mother?" His body tensed; every muscle contracted and then slowly relaxed. The color drained from his skin. He looked at Sal. With distant lights flickering in his eyes he tightened his grip on Sal's hand.

-4-

-The Bear Story-

"The best way of being kind to bears
is not being very close to them"
Margaret Atwood

The year was 1968. It would become lore in our family's history. Stories have been told over the years since that fateful night when we were visited by a wayward bear. Everyone seems to have their own personal version of the event. Some will read mine and say, "That's not exactly how it went." I know personally, that as I've heard the story retold over the years, I've often looked at the person sharing their story with a quizzical eye. They seemed to remember things I never noticed or, perhaps, that never happened. And they often leave out or confuse parts of the story that are somehow burned in my memory. I admit up front, full disclosure, that my memory of the "bear story", as we would come to refer to it, is rooted in the mind of a young boy that would be turning nine in just a few short weeks. My "bear story" is from my perspective. I'm sure there will be details overlooked and elements left out. Parts of it have, no doubt, been influenced by other's telling of the story. There may even be gaps that my young imagination (and now my old one) filled in to help the story flow. That's how stories are. They take on a life of their own. They grow and change over time, just like us. They shape us. They define us. They help mark our place in the universe. They are milestones in our journey. They remind us where we came from and what we are a part of. For better or worse, this is my "bear story".

It was a happy time in my life. It seemed so innocent. Maybe that's just how life seems to children. I had no concept of the radical changes that would be coming in a few short years. Some, sadly, had already begun, several weeks earlier with the assassination of Dr. Martin Luther King, Jr. The chaos of the sixties would usher in the seismic social changes of the seventies. Things would be radically different.

For now, from my young perspective, life was as good as it gets. It was the end of May. School was almost over. It was nearly summer; hands down, the most exciting time of year. There would be many trips down to the bayou to go fishing and swimming. In fact, back then, most of our fishing trips somehow turned into swimming trips. It was inevitable. Whatever adventures the summer might bring would pale in comparison to the day our world stood still. The day the bear came.

We lived on a small road off of Bayou Liberty Road, just outside of Slidell, Louisiana. Our road, Reis Lane, bore the last name of one of my uncles (I never did know how that came about. It just was). It wasn't much of a road back then. The parish would come out, occasionally, to cover it with a fresh load of either gravel or oyster shells. They would do their best to grade it smooth; concealing as many well-worn potholes as they could in the process. My dad, Bert, said they only came out close to election time. I was too young to notice, or care. I did always notice, however, that the potholes, somehow, always returned.

There were only a couple of families that lived on our street back then. My Aunt and Uncle, with a young platoon of my cousins, figured prominent amongst them. My Aunt's name was Rosemary. Everyone called her "Ro". My Uncle's name was Earl. Everyone called him "Bummy." My mom, Noel, often told us that her brother got his nickname from "bumming" around with the older kids. They intended it to be derogatory. Instead, it became a term of endearment. In fact, years later, his son-in-laws would jokingly, and lovingly, refer to him as "Saint Bummy".

We lived at the very end of Reis Lane. The road looped back around through our front yard. We considered it all to be our driveway. I'm sure the parish would have disagreed. The center of our front yard was dominated by an ancient oak tree. Its sprawling branches were the only jungle gym we ever had. Each child on our block became proficient in climbing it. We often held timed races to see who could traverse its breadth the quickest. It was somewhat of a badge of honor.

Once, my dad strung a cable from the tree to a large fence post. It was angled down across our yard. He placed a small metal pipe on the cable. He made me work with him setting it up. I kept asking him what it was for. He would just smile. I had no idea what we were building, until after it was stretched tight and secured. He slid the pipe back up towards the tree. "Grab ahold of it," he said. He lifted me up and I grabbed it with both hands. When he let me go, I rapidly slid down the cable with a gleeful yell. It wasn't long before everyone was lining up for a chance to ride. I think we eventually wore that cable out.

Sometimes, my dad wrapped a chain around one of the larger branches to pull an engine from an old truck. Every year he would hoist a wooden single tree up it. It signaled the end of days for one, or more, of our cows, or pigs.

My family moved from Metairie, Louisiana in the mid 1960's. It seemed that the city no longer approved of the Welsh pony, named "Doc", which we had corralled beside our house. My folks bought my grandparent's house on Reis Lane. It came with a large piece of land. On it we raised a couple of cows, several pigs, chickens, and ducks. We had a horse or two over the years as well. One, named "Chief", put me in the hospital near the end of my freshman year in high school (but that would be years from now). There was also a goat that had the misfortune of encountering the bear during his legendary visit. It did not go so well for the goat. More about that later.

A large portion of our land was dedicated to gardening. It was a small garden by any industrial standards. A very large one when compared to a typical suburban garden. In the center of our pasture, my dad built a pond. It was not very big, maybe only twenty-five or thirty feet in diameter. He chose the spot that had been my grandparent's "burn pile". Needless to say, there was a lot of debris and trash that needed to be hauled away. The pond wasn't very deep. My dad hoped it would fill with rainwater on its own, over time. That never happened. It seemed destined to only have a couple of feet of water in the bottom of it. That is, until

Hurricane Camille paid us a visit. She filled that pond to overflowing in no time. Once it was full, it pretty well stayed that way. My dad had dreams of it becoming a fish pond. He tried to stock it with any fish that survived the trip to our house from wherever he caught it. It seemed like very small perch were the only ones that took to being transplanted. I pulled many of them out of that pond over the years. I would almost always just throw them back, in hopes of catching them again. It was the closest thing to a video game I had. Sometimes, my dog, Lucky, would scarf up any rebellious perch that slipped out of my hands. But, that's a story for another time.

The pond eventually became our duck pond. My dad built a large duck house beside it. It was several feet off the ground. I only mention it now because its roof was one of our goat's favorite spots. He loved jumping up on it. His hooves would clink on the tin roof. He would jump up one side and then down the other. That duck house would prove to be somewhat of a fatal attraction for our poor goat.

Nestled between our two houses were the Lapicolas. They were an elderly couple with two daughters: Shirley and Gina. Shirley was an adult, by all rights, but she had severe developmental issues. Our worlds rarely collided. Gina was around my age. She had one major deficit, as far as I was concerned back then, she was a girl. My feelings on that matter would eventually change. For the moment, however, I was awash in a sea of girls. I didn't need to add one more to the mix.

I had five sisters: Roslyn, Kim, Tammy, Joanie, and Kathy. The only other boy on the street was my older cousin, Earl. He was almost four years older than me. Still, we stuck together as much as we could during those days. We were all that each other had in the daily battle of the sexes. Everyone called him "Toot". I think it had something to do with a children's book he loved. Toot had it even worse than I did in the girl department. He had six sisters: Suzie, Tina, Judy, Vicky, Joanne, and Loretta. They would eventually add Angie to the list, but that would be long after the bear's visit.

In fairness, there was one other boy on the street. Toot's youngest sibling, Ricky. The night that the bear arrived Ricky was less than a year old. If he tells you he remembers any of it, just smile and nod your head.

The day before the bear came was a fairly typical one in our lives. Uncle Bum invited everyone to his house for a crawfish boil. He set up sawhorses on his driveway and placed sheets of plywood on them. There were buckets and buckets of delectable crawfish dumped on them throughout the day. Mixed in with the "mudbugs" were nice chunks of sausage, ears of corn, whole onions, small potatoes, and garlic cloves. Sticks of butter and bottles of ketchup were strategically placed around the tables. We ate our fill.

At the end of the row of makeshift tables was a large trash can. By the end of the day, mounds of crawfish shells were dumped into it. It was a veritable feast. That is, if you like crawfish. Thankfully we all did. None more than my Uncle Huey. He was a machine when it came to shelling and eating crawfish. If you weren't careful, you could lose a finger if you got caught up in his machinations.

One of my favorite traditions from that time was our family jamboree sessions. Uncle Huey was somewhat of a musician during that time. We even went as far away as Bogalusa to hear him play once. I have vivid memories of him performing at the theater in what is now affectionately referred to as "Ole Towne". Back then is was just "town".

Uncle Huey would set up a couple of microphones and plug in a speaker or two. He would break out his guitar and plop a couple of notebooks on Aunt Ro's table. The notebooks were filled with handwritten copies of songs. Some of my older cousins and a couple of my uncles, would join him on their guitars. It was always "Open Mic Night" during a jamboree. All of us took turns standing in front of the family belting out our best Johnny Cash or Tammy Wynette tunes. It was "do-it-yourself-karaoke". It was a common part of our many family get-togethers. I honestly don't remember if we had a jamboree, or not, on that specific Sunday afternoon. It was such a normal part of our gatherings that I would be surprised to hear that we didn't. I like to imagine that we did. Whether we did or not, ultimately, it really didn't matter to the bear. He would be showing up long after all the instruments were put away.

That Sunday night ended like so many others during that year. We huddled around our television, with its meager five channel offering, to watch "Walt Disney's Wonderful World of Color". We drifted off to sleep, completely oblivious to the adventure waiting for us in the morning. While we slept, the bear was roaming. It was making its way towards us. Long before I woke up for school, the bear had arrived.

What happens next is pieced together from the many versions of the "bear story" I've heard over the years. I was asleep when the story started. I've taken the liberty to ad-lib a bit in order to better tell the story. I hope I don't stray too far from the actual tale.

In the early hours of the morning, Uncle Bum bolted awake. He heard a loud clanging sound in the front yard. The sound was quickly followed by a chorus of wildly barking dogs. He pressed his face against the window and looked outside to see what the commotion was all about. He strained his eyes to see. It was dark and he was still in the fog of sleep. He rubbed his eyes. *What the hell?* He couldn't believe what he was seeing. Someone had knocked over his trash can and was out there rummaging through it. He tried to make sense out of what he was seeing. He quickly remembered an encounter he had some weeks earlier with an elderly man. The old man was making a racket while he dug through the trash for any items of value. My uncle stormed outside and chided the old man for making so much noise while people were trying to sleep. The old man apologized and left with his humble gatherings.

My uncle stared out the window in disbelief. That old man was back at it again. He was making a hell of a racket. Anger rose up in him. He stormed out his bedroom and made his way to the front door. He jerked it open and hollered out at the old man "Hey!" he shouted. "What the heck are you doing?" The old man ignored him and just kept rummaging through the trash. Every dog within barking distance had shown up to serenade their disapproval at the old man. He ignored them and just kept digging. "You have got to be kidding me!" Uncle Bum leapt off the front steps and started marching towards the old man. He was going to make sure this never happened again.

Spurred on by anger, he was in a full run as he headed towards the unbelievable inconsiderate old man. "What the hell is wrong with you? People are trying to sleep!" he screamed out loud. I should mention at this point in the story that my uncle was clad in nothing but his underwear. No shoes, no shirt, no pants—just him in his tighty-whities, out to give this old man a piece of his mind.

The old man ignored him and kept scrounging in the can. Uncle Bum was livid. *Maybe he's hard of hearing?* He screamed as loud as he could, "Hey! I'm talking to you!" That seemed to get the old man's attention. He slowly backed out of the can.

Uncle Bum looked on in horror as the old man stood up. He couldn't believe what he was seeing. A giant bear was standing on its hind legs just a few feet in front of him. The bear towered over him. He was as defenseless as you can be. Armed with nothing but his underwear, he did the only reasonable thing he could think of. He turned and ran back to the house.

The bear started in after him. Several of the dogs immediately started attacking the bear. He easily swatted them away. My uncle would later declare that his dog saved his life. The diversion gave him time to make it back to house...almost. As he neared the house, Aunt Ro stepped into the open front door. She saw the dogs and the bear and jumped back. Instinctively, she slammed the front door shut and locked it.

Uncle Bum was in a fine predicament. Locked outside in his underwear with an angry bear behind him. He started banging on the door. "Rosemary! Rosemary! Let me in!" he pleaded. "Open the door!"

When she finally let him back in, he rushed to get his shotgun. It was a pretty old one. He kept it loaded with a small bird shot, mostly to keep wild dogs and coons away from his chicken pen. He grabbed the gun and completely forgot to change the shell to something bigger. He rushed back out to the bear. It was his turn to save his dog.

Against his better judgement, he made his way back out to the bear. The dogs were doing their best to hold it at bay. He often talked about how the bear was swatting dogs left and right. When he got as close to the bear as he dared, he pressed the old shotgun up close and tight against his shoulder. The bear seemed to sense what was about to happen. It stretched itself to its full height. It extended its front legs high into the air and let out a vicious roar. Uncle Bum held his breath and pulled the trigger. Bird shot or not, the sound was deafening.

The noise of the gun probably frightened the bear more than it hurt him. The bear lunged frantically to its right. A very large pine tree was only a couple of feet away. It extended its claws and reached as high as it could. It sunk those terrible claws into the side of the pine tree and shot up that tree as fast, and as high, as it could. For years afterwards, those claw marks remained. A visible testimony to the "bear story", etched into the side of the tree, a good eight feet off the ground.

The bear disappeared into the top of the tree. My uncle nervously circled the base of the tree. It was at least three feet in diameter. It was hard to see the bear in the darkness. He needed to get a flashlight. He rushed back inside. As he searched for his flashlight, a mischievous idea ran through his mind. In spite of his current level of excitement, it made him laugh to think about it. He threw some clothes on and decided to give my mom, his kid sister, a call. He snickered to himself as he waited for her to pick up.

My mom heard the phone. It was a wall mounted rotary phone located in our hallway. She got out of bed and made her groggy way towards the ringing demon. She looked at her watch. It wasn't even four yet. *Who could be calling now?* She picked up the phone and muttered a very tired, "Hello?"

"Noel!"

"Bummy? Is that you? What's going on?"

"You still got that B-B gun?"

She thought for a moment, trying to get the neurons to start firing. *B-B Gun? Oh, that's right. Behind the front door. For the chickens.* "Yeah. Why?"

"Something's messing with my chickens." He chuckled to himself.

"OK, give me a minute." She hung up the phone and quickly got dressed. She grabbed a flashlight and her B-B Gun. It was a short walk in the cool morning to his house. When she got there he was standing underneath the large pine tree in his front yard. His flashlight was on; pointed down at the ground.

"What's up?" she asked. "Something after your chickens?"

He could barely hold back the grin. He simply nodded and pointed up the tree. She looked up, thinking that maybe it was a coon. She couldn't see anything and shrugged her shoulders. He shined his flashlight up into the tree. When she saw it, she couldn't believe her eyes. A huge bear was sitting on a large limb near the top of the tree.

He shared the story with my mom. He was very animated. Neither of them could believe they were standing beneath a bear in his front yard. After a while they started to wonder what they should do. Should we just wait for it to eventually come down? That might be dangerous. The kids would be getting up soon. One of them suggested that they call the Sheriff. They'll know what to do.

They headed inside and made the call. Aunt Ro had coffee going for them. A sleepy deputy picked up the phone. He listened to their ridiculous story, certain that they were drunk. He could hear Noel in the background chiming in. He swore and then hung up on them. "He hung up on me," Bummy said incredulously.

"Call him back!" Noel said.

Bummy spun the numbers again and waited for the deputy to answer. He barely got into his story and the deputy hung up again. "What the hell?" Bummy said.

"Call him back!"

He did and once again the deputy hung up on them. He didn't have

71

any patience for drunks or prank calls. My uncle was persistent. He called again. The deputy was angry now. He threatened them, "I will come and personally arrest the both of you!"

"Good!" my uncle said, "somebody needs to come and do something about this bear." The deputy started to think that they might not be drunk. He dispatched a patrol.

Not long after I got up, about six-thirty, my mom told us all about what happened. I skipped breakfast, got dressed as fast as I could, and ran down to Uncle Bum's. There were several Sheriff Cars in the road. I got my first glimpse of the bear before I made it all the way there. I could easily make it out in the top of the tree. It was the biggest bear I had ever seen. Well, the ONLY bear I had ever seen. A couple of officers were milling around the bottom of the tree, all looking up. As I got close, I overheard their conversation. They were all encouraging each other to shimmy up the tree and see if they could get that bear to come down. "You could use a donut!" one of them said. "Coax it right out of that tree." They were all nervously laughing. It was obvious to my young mind that none of them had any intention, whatsoever, of climbing that tree. It was all good-hearted ribbing.

By eight o'clock, the bear was comfortably sitting on a couple of large branches and eating pine cones. He seemed oblivious to the crowd forming below him. Word quickly spread about the bear. Our little shelled road swelled to overflowing with spectators. Two news film crews showed up in fancy vans. Several newspaper reporters made their way through the crowds. Reports estimated that over five hundred people filled our little street to see the bear. I remember looking at all the people and wondering what they'd do if that bear came down. I imagined people would be running everywhere.

Good news for us kids, our parents said, "No school today!" We were thrilled! Except for cousin Toot. He had a field trip scheduled that day and he wasn't about to miss it. I watched him make his lonely way through the crowd of people towards the bus stop at the end of our street. For the life of me I could not imagine why he did that. It was an easy decision to me, stay home in the midst of the most excitement any of us had ever seen or go to a school event. Not even a close call.

The sheriff had a huddle with his deputies and my uncle. I pressed up as close to them as I could get. I wanted to know what was going on. Basically, nobody really knew what to do. There were still no takers on the donut option. So, they decided to call the Game Warden. About an hour later the crowd parted and the game warden drove in. He got out and was quickly briefed by the Sheriff. He walked around the tree a minute or two. He studied the bear from several angles and then slowly walked back to his truck. He dug in the back and pulled out a huge case. All eyes were on him. He took out a giant rifle. You could hear murmurs across the crowd. I watched him put a dart into it and push the bolt forward.

The Sheriff looked at him and asked, "You seriously gonna tranq that thing?" He shook his head. "What if he falls?"

The Game Warden looked up at the Sheriff. "What if he comes down that tree and attacks one of these people?" His words struck a nerve with the Sheriff. It was as though nobody had thought of that yet.

The crowd pulled back from the tree as the Sheriff shouted, "Everyone back! Get back!"

The Game Warden propped the rifle on the hood of his truck. He wrapped the strap tightly around his left hand and took aim. Seconds slowly ticked by as everyone waited. It was deathly silent when he fired. Direct hit! You could actually see the little yellow dart hanging in the bear's back. It swatted at it but didn't seem to be bothered by it too much. He reloaded and shot it again. Another hit.

The Game Warden said, "Now we wait." About three or four minutes passed and the bear started swaying. It clawed at the tree and then fell forward, unconscious. Everybody cheered. Then the bear started to slump. You could hear gasps in the crowd. The bear was coming down! It was going to fall. After a few unsteady seconds, it started to tumble down the tree. You could have heard a pin drop as everyone watched it bounce from one branch to another. After it had fallen several feet, in what seemed like slow motion, the bear came to rest across two large branches.

Its front and rear legs hung straight down. Its head rested comfortably on the front branch. It was basically stuck up there now; comfortably napping. It wouldn't be falling any time soon. Stifled laughter broke out across the crowd.

Now what? Again, the deputies started talking about climbing the tree and pushing the bear out. No takers. Somebody in the crowd spoke up and said there was a cherry picker working the power lines a couple of blocks over. Maybe they could help. The Sheriff dispatched a deputy and in about fifteen minutes here it came. Meanwhile, the bear enjoyed a nice nap. A "cherry picker" was one of those large trucks that electric companies used to work on power lines. It had a large bucket on the end of a crane. A person could get in it and ride up to a transformer to work on it.

The men were very excited to be called into action. I'm sure none of them had ever done anything like this before. They got the truck as close as they could to the tree. One man slowly extended the bucket to its maximum reach. It was about eight to ten feet too short. Now what?

The Sheriff asked the man if he could shake the tree with the bucket. He said he'd give it a try. People started asking, "What's gonna happen to the bear? Will the bear be all right?" They didn't seem too happy with the Sheriff's idea of just shaking the bear out of the tree.

The bucket operator said, "Let me try something." He put the bucket directly under the bear and started pushing it against the tree. After a couple of minutes of pushing the tree, the bear started to move. It started falling head first—slow at first and then it began to slide. The operator quickly lined the bucket up and the bear fell right into the bucket head first—still unconscious. The crowd really cheered now.

They moved the bucket over to the Game Warden's truck. It took a little maneuvering, but after several minutes they were able to tip the bucket at just the right angle. The bear slid out and dropped into the bed of the truck. It filled up the back of that truck.

Everyone rushed in for a closer look. All of the deputies moved in.

After they were sure the bear was out for the count, they all took turns taking photos with the bear. The Game Warden called my Uncle over and showed him the spot where he shot the bear. I leaned in close. The Game Warden brushed his fingers through the bear's hair and tiny little B-B's flicked off. None of them even penetrated the bear's skin. I reached in and ran my fingers through the bear's fur. I placed my hand against its massive paws. I ran my fingers up against its claws. I can still see those claws when I close my eyes.

The Game Warden said he was taking the bear to Honey Island Swamp to be relocated. We made front page news the next morning. There was a picture with my Uncle Johnny, staring up at the camera, standing beside the truck, with the bear sprawled out in the bed. We were also on a couple of local TV stations. It was pretty exciting. Ten years later, the town newspaper did an anniversary piece on the story. Uncle Bum kept the original newspaper story framed in his living room. Hanging from the side of the frame, on a white string, was the shotgun shell.

After the bear was taken away, after the crowds dispersed, we made our way back home. It was only then that we discovered some more damage done by the bear. The gate leading to our pasture had been knocked down. The bear had apparently come out of the woods behind our pasture, no doubt lured out by the smell of the crawfish shells in Uncle Bum's trash can. As I made my way into our pasture, I passed the duck cages. You could see the bear's tracks pressed into the dirt. It had clearly come through here. If there was any doubt, on top of the duck cage, right in the path of the bear, was our goat. It just laid there, unmoving. It didn't take me long to realize that it was dead. I examined its body for any clues and found none. My dad theorized that the goat ran up there to get away from the bear and then died of a heart attack. It made sense to me at the time. I felt sorry for that goat. It really did enjoy jumping up on that duck cage.

To this day, whenever we all get back together, we all love to tell and retell the story about the night the bear came to visit. The story has grown and blossomed over the years. And to this day, nobody tells a better "bear story" than Uncle Bum.

POSTSCRIPT

After writing this story, to best of my recollections, I came across the original newspaper clipping. Mostly, I wanted to just confirm the date. I have to be honest, when I saw the picture, I was surprised at how small the bear seemed to me now. It was still a very large black bear. It was as long as the truck bed, but it only filled up half of its width. In my mind, it was a giant grizzly. Also interesting, the article said the bear was eighty feet up in the tree. I remembered it being much closer. I guess I focused on where it came to rest, about thirty feet up. Like I said, stories grow and change, our mind shapes and forms them over the years. I'm a little disappointed that the bear wasn't as massive as I remembered. Still, it was pretty scary, and very dangerous. It was after all, a full-grown black bear. A formidable foe for anyone armed with only a loose-fitting pair of underwear.

-5-

-Virginia Dare-

"Behold, I show you a mystery; We shall not all sleep,
but we shall all be changed,"
Saint Paul, I Corinthians 15:51

Cordelia watched the hazy figure making its way across the ridgeline, gliding through the snow. She couldn't make out who it was, but she was certain it wasn't one of the men folk. They weren't due back from the meeting for two more days, at the earliest. Besides, the figure looked too small to be one of the men. Whoever it was walked alone. No mule. No pack. That meant they had to be coming from somewhere close—maybe the other side of the holler? She'd have to wait till they got closer.

Cordelia placed another log on the fire and then hung the kettle over the flames. Whoever it was would surely appreciate a nice hot cup of coffee after a long, cold trek. *Wonder what they want? Why would anybody come out in this weather? Must be pretty serious.*

Cordelia slid the stool up next to the fireplace. She stepped up and pulled the heavy musket rifle from its rack. *Best not take any chances.* She went to the window and rubbed the ice off with her sleeve. She was shocked at how close the figure was now. Only a couple of hundred yards away now. Close enough to see that it was a young girl. Cordelia asked out loud, "Who is that fool girl? She ain't even got on a jacket or a hat! She is gonna freeze to death for sure!" She hollered up to the loft, "Josiah, get down here, right now. No time to waste boy, get down here!"

The sleepy nine year old boy slid down the ladder as ordered, "Yes Mam?"

77

"Josiah, you run quick and get the ladies."

"All of 'em?"

"Yes, all of 'em. Now go boy, tell 'em we got a girl in trouble coming in from the snow. Go! And you be quick!"

Cordelia stepped out on the porch. The girl seemed to glide through the snow with no effort at all. *Are her legs even moving? I can't quite tell, her dress is blowing too much.* The girl was close enough now for Cordelia to see that all she had on was a simple white dress. It was way too thin to be wearing in this weather. It seemed to flow into the falling snow. Hard to see where one ended and the other began. *What's that in her hair?* Cordelia strained to see. *Flowers? Where'd she get flowers this time of year? And why's she got 'em all braided in her hair like that?*

Cordelia scrutinized the girl. *She looks like she done dressed up for a Spring Dance or something.* She seemed to be lost in a trance. *She must be in shock or near dead!* The girl didn't even seem to notice the snow or freezing temperatures. Cordelia laid the musket against the wall. She wrapped Jameson's big elk coat around her and stepped out towards the girl.

"What are you doing out here girl?" she hollered as she stepped out into the snow. The girl didn't seem to hear her. She was focused on something in the distance. Cordelia trudged through the snow until she was in line with the girl. The girl was only about thirty feet or so from her now. Even though she was heading straight for her, she didn't seem to notice Cordelia at all. Cordelia waved her arms and screamed out, "You! Girl! Can you hear me? What in God's name are you doing out here?" she asked as the girl floated towards her. "Are you lost? Are you from the holler? Is your family in trouble? Why are you out here girl?"

The girl finally seemed to notice Cordelia. She stopped about ten feet from her and stared. Cordelia studied the girl in her thin white dress. She wasn't shivering. She didn't even seem to be cold. Her blonde hair was blowing in the wind. Cordelia looked down and was shocked to see that the girl was barefoot. Even stranger, she was standing on dirt. Cordelia looked back down at her own feet. They were a good three or four inches under the snow. *How is that possible?* she wondered. She glanced behind the girl, expecting to see footprints in the snow. Instead, the girl had left a clear path through the snow. It was as though the snow melted away beneath her. Cordelia was confused. She looked back up at the girl, not knowing what to make of all this. The young girl smiled at her. Cordelia took a step back, suddenly frightened. The girl stepped towards her. Cordelia watched in fear and amazement as the snow simply disappeared around the girl's feet. It didn't melt. It just disappeared. *This is wrong. Wrong!* her brain screamed.

Fresh snow was still falling. Cordelia lifted her arms and saw that she was already covered with a fine light mist. She looked back at the girl. She didn't have any snow on her at all—none. "Who are you?" Cordelia asked in barely a whisper. The girl reached out her hand. Part of Cordelia wanted to recoil in horror. Instead, she instinctively reached out her hand in response. Worlds collided when their hands touched. A jolt ran through Cordelia. Heat exploded through her body. The snow turned into instant steam as it touched her. Her mind raced with images and sounds. Swirling colors filled her eyes.

"Lay her gently," Cordelia heard a voice echo in her mind. She felt trembling hands under her—softly, ever so softly, laying her down against the cold hard stone. *A cave? Is this a cave? What is that light?* Warmth pulsed through her back. The cold stone began to hum softly. Something searching, seeking, probing, hoping—and then finding....filling her...rocking her...*Sleep child, shhhhh, just rest and sleep. We'll watch over you.* The light faded and darkness enveloped her. Her soul rested in the glowing light and the glowing light rested in her. Time stopped and yet she moved on. Children became parents and parents became dust, as the girl slept in the warmth of the stone. Ancient mysteries filled her with silent wonder. She was one with the light and the light was one with her. Together they rested and grew. Together they dreamed and hoped. Together they longed for the time of wakening and sharing—and now it was here!

Cordelia gasped and pulled her hand back. The girl collapsed in a heap just as the women came running through the snow.

"Who is that girl, Cordelia?" Sarai, the oldest, asked.

Cordelia turned to face the women. All four of them had come. This was good. The light would be pleased. "Her name is Virginia," Cordelia said. "Virginia Dare."

-6-

-Time and Time Again-

"For this corruptible must put on incorruption,
and this mortal must put on immortality."
Saint Paul, I Corinthians 15:53

Quentin Tell bolted upright in bed gasping for air. Fear coursed through his body. His eyes darted around the room. *Where the hell am I?* A flash of lightning overwhelmed his senses. He closed his eyes to concentrate, to shut it out all out. He wanted to stay blissfully unconscious, but the thunder bouncing around inside his head wasn't about to let that happen. Slowly, ever so slowly, he opened his eyes. He was home, in his own bed. How the hell he got there, he had no idea. Not surprising, considering the party. *The party!* He turned and surveyed the other side of the bed. He was alone. *Damn! What went wrong?*

Debbie, from accounting, had been all over him, as was Carol, as was Stella. The partners threw a huge impromptu party. They had reason to celebrate. They had just won the biggest case in the firm's history. Bonuses flowed as freely as the alcohol. Tell was especially jubilant. His hefty bonus was being followed up with a much coveted promotion. He was meeting with the partners tomorrow morning to be welcomed into the fold. Tonight, like all the rest of the firm, he partied. And how he partied!

This was his night. The universe revolved around him. And he would relish every moment of it. He would party his ass off! Then he would collapse into a drunken euphoria in the arms of some nice delectable treat. Could life get any better than that? Everything was perfect. Yet, he couldn't shake the nagging sensation that somehow, it had all turned out wrong.

He thought back over the evening. The only sour note he could think of was that little fiasco with Sean Jacobs. God, how he hated that

81

scumbag! Jacobs was always coming in at the last minute, and taking credit for everyone else's work. Even tonight, after he had invested a considerable amount of time into their lovely secretary, Tammy—Jacobs swooped in at the last minute and that was the last he saw of her. She was primed for the picking. Tell did the priming and Jacobs did the picking. Oh well, there was still Debbie, Carol, and Stella. Tell searched his brain for an answer to the mystery of how, with those odds, he still wound up home alone. He was convinced that somehow Jacobs was involved. That was alright. With a devious smirk on his face, Tell made a commitment to use his new promotion to help the young Mr. Jacobs find a successful career somewhere else. Yeah, payback was coming. But first, he had to take a leak.

Tell noticed a steady pulse of light and glanced to his left. The clock on his desk was flashing, 2:32. *Great!* he thought, *I guess the lights went out in the storm.* He rolled his feet over the side of the bed and sat up. He felt like crap on a stick. He staggered towards the bathroom, feeling the full weight of the hangover he had so rightfully earned. He didn't even bother turning on the lights, he just lifted the lid of the toilet and aimed out of habit. He would let the maid worry about his accuracy tomorrow. *Hell, what time is it anyway?* he wondered. Tell raised his watch in front of his face. He squinted blood shot eyes to make out the numbers. Surely that's not right? How can that be possible? He rubbed his eyes to improve his focus and tried again. No doubt about it, his watch declared the time to be "2:32" as well. "What the hell is going on?" Tell said. "Did the lights *just* go out?"

He turned to leave and a wave of dizziness flooded his body. He grabbed the edge of the sink to steady himself. It felt like his mind and his stomach were at odds about which would leave his body first. An odd array of colors and sounds seemed to engulf him. Tell had earned his share of frat-house merit badges in college. On more than one occasion he had drunk himself into oblivion. And like all drunks, the day after being the life of the party, he had hell to pay. This was different. This seemed to be twisting his brain, with spinal cord attached, right out of his body like a cork screw. The sensation was both nauseating and psychotic. Thank the porcelain gods, the feeling passed.

Tell straightened up and took a deep breath. There was still a slight feeling of disconnectedness. Like his body had an "out-of-mind" experience or something. As long as there would be no puking, he guessed he could handle that. Gingerly, he made his way to the desk. The clock's steady flashing of "2:32" was beginning to irritate him. Wait a minute! At least five good minutes had passed since he first noticed the clock. Why hadn't the time gone forward? A quick glance at his watch only added to the confusion. It too seemed to be stuck on 2:32 as well. Tell held it to his ear. Nothing. A closer look revealed that the second hand was motionless. What the hell was going on? Losing electricity would explain the clock, perhaps. But the watch? What could possibly cause that? Tell wrinkled his eyebrows in a truly perplexed manner. His mind ran through a quick series of plausible explanations. Lightning! That had to be it. Somehow the lightning storm had screwed up his watch. What else could it be? Tell wondered, as he surveyed the jewel-encrusted time piece. It was beautiful. One of his prized possessions. It had been a gift from his Nana when he graduated law school. He had it appraised the very next day. He was thrilled to learn that she had paid a little over twelve thousand dollars for it. He shook his wrist. "God, I hope it ain't fried," he whispered.

Tell pulled out the stem on the watch and quickly spun it backwards until the hour and minute both lined up on the large diamond just above the "XII". Once again, he was overwhelmed with a swirl of colors and sounds. They seemed to be coming from everywhere. They wrapped around his body like a small tornado. He could feel air flowing around him as though he were being transported by the bizarre lights. The sensation made him nauseous. He was clearly moving through the air. But to where?

Before the swirling colors dissipated, the sounds came in clearer. There was music and Tell could make out people laughing and talking. The kaleidoscope of colors faded around him. He found himself standing in the midst of a very happening party. Standing isn't exactly right. It felt as though he were floating, like a disembodied spirit. Curiosity seemed to keep his fear at bay. *Where am I? What in the world is happening to me?* Tell wanted to know. A quick glance around the room answered the first question. Tell was back at the party. It was exactly as he remembered it.

But this was no memory. Tell was actually back at the party! *How can this be?*

His body floated effortlessly above the people as they danced and swayed below him. Nobody seemed to notice him at all. His right hand still held the watch stem at midnight. The large clock over the mantle agreed. A flash of red caught his eye. It was Stella. There was something electric about her. Even now, as a second-rate ghost, she excited him. Didn't they dance tonight? He seemed to remember her sliding up next to him and whispering something about being lonely into his ear. He followed her as she made her way through the crowd of people. She must have spray painted that dress on. It captured every luscious curve and detail of her body. Damn, she was gorgeous!

Tell was so enraptured by her beauty that he didn't notice he was passing through people like a whiff of smoke. He was mesmerized by those swaying hips. The back of that dress cut all the way down to the very edge of paradise. He caught himself just as he was about to run into her, or through her as the case might be. Tell pulled back and floated up towards the ceiling. His heart caught in his throat, if he still had one, as he watched her slide up next to a young man and whisper something in his ear. The man spun around. A look of surprised interest and naughty mischief filled his face. It was Tell!

He wanted to scream. He threw his hands out in front of him, releasing the watch stem. Instantly, he was back in his bedroom. His mind was reeling from the experience. He glanced over at the clock. It was still flashing, 2:32.

"What in the name of God was that?" Tell asked out loud, more out of fear than anything else. He had to sit down. Had to screw his head back on straight. He glanced at the bottle of bourbon. Was that the cure or the cause of all of this? Tell shook his head. One thing was sure. He would have to lay off the sauce for a while. At least for a few days anyway. This was crazy. It couldn't be happening. *Maybe I'm still dreaming*, he thought. He lightly slapped his own face. *Nope. Wide awake.* He hoped it wasn't some sort of psychotic episode or something. He didn't have time for that. Not now. Especially considering tomorrow. *Tomorrow! Oh God!*

He almost forgot about the meeting with the partners. He had to get some rest. The last thing he needed was to show up late for that. Even worse, he definitely didn't need to show up looking like an extra from "One Flew Over the Cuckoo's Nest".

Purely out of habit, Tell glanced down at his watch. The hands had returned to match the flashing clock's time, 2:32. *That's impossible! I didn't move them back!* He took a deep breath to steady himself. Although he didn't feel like it, Tell was becoming convinced that he must still be stone-cold drunk. He had to sleep it off. That was it! Everything would be fine with a good night's sleep. He would go to the meeting rested and refreshed. He would wow the partners. They would be impressed! They would leave the meeting knowing they had made the right choice.

"What time is that meeting anyway?" Tell asked the empty room. What he was really asking was, *How much time do I have left to sleep?* He picked up his date book from the desk and flipped it open. He thumbed through the pages until he got to tomorrow's date. Slowly he ran his finger down the page. There it was. The meeting with the partners was at 11:00. He could still get a few good hours of sleep under his belt. *I wish I knew what time it really was*, he thought. He tapped his finger on the book, holding it pressed against the 11:00 slot. Again he was overwhelmed with a swishing array of colors and sounds. The same flowing sensation surrounded him as though he were flying through air. He could feel the wind as the colors caressed his entire being. Although he seemed to be spinning like a top, it was not an unpleasant feeling. There wasn't any nausea or dizziness this time. The colors slowly gave way to soft fluorescent lighting. The sound seemed to dissipate into silence. Again, Tell found himself floating above a group of people, like an invisible cloud. The date book still in his hands; his finger firmly pressed over the 11:00 slot.

He instantly recognized the place and the people. It was the partners. They were in the firm's board room. Tell studied their silent faces. Each seemed to be absorbed in reading memos and jotting quick notes in the margins. Nobody noticed Tell floating effortlessly above the oval table. After several moments of silence, the president spoke up.

"Where the hell is he?" the man asked.

"He'll be along shortly sir," someone answered.

"He did know the meeting was at 11:00 right?" the man asked, clearly agitated.

"Yes sir, he did," the same person responded.

"Well, where the hell is he?" he asked as he glanced at his watch.

Yes, where the hell am I? Tell wondered. *I should be here. There is no way in the world I would miss this meeting. Where am I?* Again, Tell squirreled up his eyebrows as his brain contemplated various scenarios. While not an avid fan, Tell had read his fair share of Sci-Fi. His mind did a random search for any "time travel" information it could find. All the books and movies he was familiar with seemed to say that two bodies can't be in the same place at the same time.

"That's it!" Tell said in a very assured voice. "I can't be here, because I'm already here!" Somehow it made sense to him as he floated above the boardroom ala Casper-the-ghost, watching tomorrow's meeting before it even happened. Tell looked down at the date book in his hand. Deliberately he lifted his finger off the book. Instantly he was back in the bedroom.

"This just gets weirder and weirder!" He threw the book on the desk and began to pace the room. "Think Tell! Think!" He demanded to himself. After several minutes of pacing back and forth, running his hands through his hair, he came to two possible explanations.

"Alright, either I'm still sleeping it off or something happened when that lightning hit." He slapped his face as hard as he could, with both hands this time. "Ow!" he responded instantly. So much for the former. It had to be the latter. That was the only logical conclusion. Something bizarre happened to him. Somehow the storm had turned him into a one-man time machine. Oh yeah, there was also the outside chance he could simply be bat-shit crazy. There was one simple way to confirm his theory.

He held the watch in front of himself and pulled out the stem. He spun the hands backwards until they aligned themselves over the XII. Instantly the colors rushed over him in a tidal wave of sights and sounds. As they cleared he was once again floating above a crowd of people. The clock on the mantle declared that it was midnight. Again, a flash of red caught his eye as Stella began to weave and sway through the crowd toward her intended target, Quentin Tell. As much as he wanted to watch her every motion, Tell released the watch and instantly found himself standing back in the bedroom.

"Alright, at least I'm not nuts," he said to himself in a reassuring tone. He tried to sort this out in his mind. What could this mean? Was it a permanent condition? Could he time travel at will?

"I wonder," he said as he picked up the date book. Tell flipped the book open to a random date. His finger fell over a note written for a lunch date with a client about two months ago. Tell steadied himself and pressed his finger down onto the book. The colors enveloped him in a brisk and soothing manner. The wind rushed around him. The sounds seemed to be singing. The sensation was rather enjoyable this time. As things cleared, Tell was floating near the ceiling of a very nice Italian restaurant. Two people were sitting at the table directly below him. One of them was a no-count contractor trying desperately to beat two charges of fraud. The other was the up and coming lawyer, Quentin Tell. He scanned the restaurant. Everything was exactly as he remembered it. All in all, it was a fairly boring lunch. Tell lifted his finger from the date book and instantly returned to the bedroom.

Now he was energized! This could be fun! For the next several hours Tell floated back and forth between his past appointments and his bedroom with the ease of a genie. Each time he returned, the clock continued to flash 2:32. Screw the clock! Twice he went back to one particularly memorable engagement with the seductively attractive Debbie, from accounting. That girl was an animal! Yes, this could turn out to be even better than getting free Pay-Per-View!

What about the future? Tell wondered. He quickly flipped the book ahead to a couple of key appointments a few weeks out. The meeting with that heiress jumped out at him. That case was going to make him another huge bonus. He had to see how this one turned out. Tell pressed his finger against the book. He welcomed the warm embrace of the colors and the soothing melody of the sounds as the brisk air flowed around him. He was in the receiving room of her elaborate estate. She sat in a large leather chair with her hands folded across her lap. Exquisite art and priceless antiques surrounded her. The very setting was a testimony to her immense fortune. *She probably has no idea how much she's worth*, Tell thought as he floated silently above her. Too bad about her husband's tragic accident. *Shit happens*, he thought. Then, *Business was business and money was money*. And there was a ton of money to be made if he played his cards right.

The butler entered the room and announced in a monotone voice, "Your lawyer is here madam." Tell turned to watch himself walk into the room.

"Mr. Jacobs," the old lady said as she rose from her seat.

He was stunned into disbelief. This quickly gave way to red-hot anger. Sean Jacobs had stolen his client! Who the hell did he think he was? He was filled with killer rage. That back-stabbing S.O.B.! How could the firm let him get away with this? There was no way in the world that Tell was going let this happen. He would do everything in his power to get Jacobs fired as quickly as possible. This was all wrong! This is not how it's supposed to happen! Tell couldn't stand another second of this nonsense. He jerked his finger off the book and rushed back to his bedroom.

"That doesn't make sense," he said.

He considered another brisk trip, or two, back to his rendezvous with Debbie, just to put himself in a better mood. Instead he flipped through the date book to find another key appointment. *Aha! The budget meeting with the whole team.* He would be leading that one. Again, holding the date book in his left hand, he pressed his right index finger down on the time. Swirling colors and melodic sounds encased him. The rushing wind seemed to soothe his anxious spirit. Slowly, the fog of the colors and sounds misted away and he was floating effortlessly above the small conference room. The meeting was in full session. Folders, notebooks, and calculators seemed to be everywhere. Everyone seemed to be talking at once. Each person was taking a stand for their expenses or their pet project. That's what he loved about these types of meetings. They were ferocious. Everyone was territorial. This was war! And he was in his element.

Debbie was staring aimlessly out the window. She had a deep, pensive look on her face. That's not what caught his eye, however. "Dear God! Look at the cleavage!" Tell whistled as he took in the ample flowing hills of Debbie's landscape. This alone was worth the trip. He was prematurely jerked out of his Zen moment when a loud voice boomed from the head of the table. Jacobs was in his seat!

"Alright, settle down people! Remember, I set the priorities. You make them work. It's that simple," Jacobs said with a smile.

Tell screamed his silent rage to the heavens, "Don't listen to him! Jacobs is a jerk! This is my meeting! Not his!" He flew at Jacobs in a violent swoop. There was no impact. No resistance. No sound. No effect. He simply passed right through him.

He snatched his finger off the book and stood quietly in his lonely bedroom. Tell took in several deep, slow breaths. He wanted to explode. How could he make sense of this? Why would Jacobs be doing his work? Why would they give Jacobs his job? His cases? Then it hit him. Of course! The promotion! That had to be it. That explains everything. Jacobs wasn't doing "his job". Jacobs was working for him! The very thought of if it filled Tell with a wonderful sense of gleeful vengeance. "Oh yeah! I am going to make your life a living hell Jacobs!" He burst into laughter at the very thought of it. He would use his new found talent to spy on him. He would always be one step ahead of Jacobs now. The possibilities and the pleasures were endless. Tell exhaled. A sense of deep satisfaction filled him. Life was good. Aside from waking up in bed alone, this had been a delightfully wonderfully evening. It would only get better.

Tell gently laid the book back on the desk. *I have got to get some sleep,* he thought wearily. His eyes were drawn back to the flashing clock. It was still stuck on its monotonous time of 2:32. Tell looked at his watch, ditto. Time travel aside, this was most perplexing. How is it that time seemed to be standing still? The answers evaded him.

"I wonder what would happen," Tell said out loud as he raised his finger over the face of the watch. "Only one way to find out." He pressed his finger against the watch. The swirling colors bathed him in a glorious fury that approached ecstasy. The sounds seemed to vibrate through every fiber of his being in a glorious harmony. Tell was lost in the sensation. It swallowed his anxiety and confusion. He wanted this moment to last forever. For those few seconds, all was right in the universe. The colors began to melt away as the sights and sounds of the room came into sharp focus.

Tell was hovering softly near the ceiling of a small, well-lit room. A team of frantic doctors and nurses were furiously engaged in caring for a patient. Something about that patient seemed both familiar and strangely foreign to him. Everything was confusing. The young man lying on the hospital bed was completely motionless. A nervous doctor yelled "Again!"

Someone thrust two paddles onto the young man's exposed chest. He raised his head and hollered out, "Clear!" The young man's body arched off the bed for a brief moment. All eyes turned to the monitor. Nothing.

"Again!" the doctor yelled.

"Clear!" the one with the paddles declared. The jolt was evident as the body on the table jerked upward.

All eyes turned back to the monitor. Nothing. A tear flowed down the cheek of the disembodied Tell.

"Alright. That's it," the lead physician said to his team. Disappointment covered his face. He ripped the latex gloves off his hands. "Mark it!" he said out loud. "Time of death, 2:32."

Tell looked down in utter dismay. An odd mixture of grief, sorrow, and peace seemed to engulf him. He glanced down at his own broken body. Already they were pulling the sheet over his head. *Is this it? Is this how it ends?* Although the answer seemed painfully obvious, Tell refused to accept it. "I have too much to live for!" he objected to whomever, or whatever, might be listening.

Tell watched, this time in horror, as the swirling colors began to form below him. Like a small tornado, they began to pull him downward. It was clear to him that they meant to suck him from this dimension to the next. He panicked and quickly shot to the other side of the room. The colors opened into a spiraling tube. Soothing sounds beckoned to him from the other side. Tell watched in deep fascination as the other end of the tube of light began to slowly open. A glorious white light reached out to him. Its warmth urged him towards it. "So this is what it's like?" Tell asked softly. He began to drift towards light. The sounds seemed to consume his very being. It was peaceful beyond description. Nothing mattered except for the light. Everything within him wanted to go towards it. Not even Jacobs could screw this moment up for him.

Jacobs! Tell stopped at the edge of the pulsing light. If he "crossed over" that would mean that Jacobs won. Jacobs gets his job, his promotion, and all the benefits that came with it. His mind filled with the sensuous image of Stella's swaying hips. "There is no way in hell that Jacobs gets it all! I'll be damned if I let that happen!"

The sense of peace and comfort was shattered by Tell's sudden outburst of anger. He stopped floating just over the very edge of the tube of light. A simple push and he would enter its eternal peace. Somehow he knew this. There was no doubt in his mind. It called to him. The sound of it was intoxicating. It was slowly washing his anger away. In a moment, Sean Jacobs would no longer matter. Nothing would.

In understanding that exceeded words, Tell knew that he had two choices. He could surrender to the light and be washed in its eternal peace and comfort. All the cares and concerns of this life would be gone. He could rest in eternal bliss. Or not.

In direct defiance to the light's offer, Tell coldly and deliberately lifted his finger from the watch. Instantly he was back in his bedroom. The clock still flashing 2:32. Somehow, Tell would figure a way out of this. He would fix things. After all, he was one of the best lawyers in the firm, he would find a loophole. If there was any way out of here, he would find it. He had to. He had no other options. He would do everything in his power to insure that Sean Jacobs didn't take his future from him. He would travel back in time, as many times as it took, and he would make things right. Tell walked over to the table and picked up the book.

A strange glow flickered outside the window. It seemed to grow in intensity. Fear welled up in Tell's chest. A terrible noise began to build outside the room. It sounded as though an avalanche was bearing down upon him. He had to get away and quick! He flipped the book open. His eyes turned white in horror. The pages were all blank.

"No!" Tell screamed from the depths of his soul. He rushed to the window and pulled the curtains back. He fell to his knees in screaming agony as fire burst through the walls. It overwhelmed him. The flames were everywhere. The scorching heat was excruciating. Relentless groans and shrieks of terror rolled up from its depth. He turned away from the flames. Tell watched in pitiful horror as the silent clock was consumed by the fire. Together they began to fall hopelessly towards the center of the flames. Still, it flashed, 2:32.

Mommy Too

"So also is the resurrection of the dead. It is sown in corruption; it is raised in incorruption."
Saint Paul, I Corinthians 15:42

C arol Morgan felt an uneasy presence pulling her towards the end of the hall. She inched along the edge of the wall, clinging to the shadows. She had no idea where she was. No idea how she got there. No idea what waited for her at the end of the hall. She only knew one thing: she had to get to the end of the hall. She had to walk through that door. Nothing else in the universe mattered.

Her heart pounded. Frightened beyond words, every instinct within her cried, *Turn back! Run!* Yet she stood pressed against the wall, gazing towards the end of the hall. She was trying to muster the courage to make one last bold dash for the door before they found her—whoever "they" might be.

A sharp metallic click from down the hall made her heart stop. She held her breath. She dared not move. A soft scraping sound floated down the hall. There were faint footsteps and whispers. Carol's eyes darted back and forth. Were they coming towards her? Or going away? She strained to hear. Uncertain of what to do, she did nothing. The sounds melted into silence and she breathed a sigh of relief. For the moment, she was alone. *Where am I?* She glanced down at her feet. *Where are my shoes?* Then she noticed the hospital gown. *What the hell?* She stepped away from the wall. A hospital bracelet on her right wrist confirmed that she was indeed Carol Morgan. Her name was followed by the letters "DOB". She pawed at the bracelet, spinning it to read "12/29/37".

"That's not right!" she muttered out loud. Panic seized her. She grabbed the bracelet and ripped it off her arm. "That's not right!" she screamed and threw it on the floor. A metal tray clanged to the floor. She turned to face the sound. It came from behind the door. She heard someone shout and start running towards the door. Light spilled into the hallway as the door flew open. Fear flooded through her. They were coming for her. She had to get away! She turned to run and fell into the center of the hall. Her face slammed hard into the cold tile. She laid there, pressed against the floor. The noises stopped. Should she get up and run? Should she stay where she was? She heard what could only be described as gleeful chuckling coming from behind her. She twisted her head to see. Someone, or something, was silhouetted in the door. She heard a sharp click followed by a scraping sound. She pushed herself up to run. Someone shouted, "No!" Something wrapped around her left leg and started dragging her towards the door. She screamed and began kicking.

It let go. She stood and started running. She stopped when she heard her name, "Carol! Carol Morgan!"

She started to turn when it grabbed her again. One quick jerk and she was flung back to the floor. The impact knocked the breath out of her. She clawed for something to hold on to as she was being pulled down the hall. The pain was intense but her fear held it at bay. She screamed and kicked until it finally let go. She jumped to her feet and started sprinting down the hall. She had to get away from the door, away from the pain, away from that frightening light.

"Carol! Carol Morgan!" a voice called out to her. She would not be tricked this time. She ignored the voice and kept running. She ran until her sides hurt. She ran until she couldn't run any more. The hallway seemed to go on forever. She looked for an exit, a door, a window, somewhere to hide. There was nothing. Just a long empty hall that offered no hope of escape. She stopped to catch her breath. She looked behind her. Expecting to hear footsteps getting closer, she heard nothing but deafening silence. No one was coming after her. That was a relief. She put her hands on her knees and took several deep breaths.

"Think Carol!" she demanded of herself. "Where am I? What the hell is going on?" Something caught her eye. It was in the middle of the hall about twenty feet in front of her. She walked towards it. She circled it as she glanced up and down the hall.

"Is this a joke?" she said as she picked it up. It was her hospital bracelet.

She slid down the wall and sat on the floor. *What kind of a hospital is this? Am I insane? This has to be a dream. One really screwed up dream.*

A soft voice from the other side of the wall startled her. She pushed away from it and scurried to the other side of the wall. She sat staring at the wall for several minutes. *Maybe it was just my imagination.* Then the wall spoke again.

"You have to let it happen on its own, Carol. Don't fight it. Let it happen on its own."

Carol Morgan was beaten. She was beyond being frightened. She was without options; without any hope. She pulled her knees against her chest and began to slowly rock back and forth. Eventually she rocked herself to sleep.

A sharp clicking sound startled her. She opened her eyes. She was laying on the floor against the wall in a tight fetal position. She heard footsteps and hushed whispers. She sat up when she heard that scraping noise again. It was coming from down the hall. In her hand she still held the hospital bracelet. She studied it intently, "Carol Morgan: DOB, 12/29/37".

"That's not right," she said. "I was born in August." She glanced around to see if anyone was coming. "I was born in August!" she screamed down the hall.

"August 26th, 2002, not thirty-seven! I was not born in thirty-seven!"

A grinding sound filled the air. It was coming from overhead. It sounded like someone was opening a giant jar of pickles. The voice seemed to come from everywhere. "You have to let it happen on its own

Carol. You need to just relax and let it happen on its own. You'll know when it's time."

Carol stood to run. She surveyed her options. To the left was the door. *How did I get back to the door?* To her right was a long straight hallway with no end in sight. *What's the use?* She sat back down against the wall.

"Who the hell are you people?" She screamed towards the door. "What are you doing to me? Why am I here?"

"We're here to help you, Carol" a voice replied from beyond the door.

"Help me? Why am I here? Is something wrong with me?"

"Everything is fine, Carol. Everything is alright."

"Alright? Fine? Are you insane?" She screamed at the door. "What the hell is this place? Where am I? Why is the date wrong on my bracelet?"

"You need to trust us, Carol. You need to relax. When it's time…"

She leaped to her feet and rushed towards the door with a deep primal scream. She didn't even bother with the knob. She just started banging on the door with both fists; screaming and kicking with every ounce of energy she had.

"Let me out of here! Let me out of here!"

"Carol, you need to relax. We'll talk more later. Right now you need to rest."

She heard that same scraping sound again, like a giant lid was being screwed on.

"Relax, Carol. Get some rest." The voice said from above her this time.

A feeling of weightlessness came over her. Everything went fuzzy. She felt disoriented. The walls shifted. The air seemed to slosh around her body. There was no way to fight it. She plopped down into the middle of the hall and fell into a deep, deep sleep.

Moments later, she was standing in a gorgeous meadow. A soft breeze filtered through the trees. She was standing on a well-worn path that followed beside a small stream. She scanned the horizon. She was alone. Carol turned around. There was nothing behind her. No meadow. No stream. Nothing but empty open space. *That's odd,* she thought. She turned back around. The world only seemed to be in front of her. The path began at her feet.

Carol started walking down the path. It was a beautiful day. Her soul was at peace. The path turned into a small grove of trees. Gorgeous fields of wildflowers waved in the light breeze. She stopped to listen to the stream as it babbled over the rocks. This had to be the most beautiful place she had ever been. Everything was perfect. Then she saw it. On the other side of the stream was a small metal desk. A single log was laid across the stream in front of it. Seated at the desk was a young girl. Carol watched in fascination as the young girl removed a file from an in-box. Without looking up from her work, the girl said, "Next."

Carol turned around. She was the only other person there. The little girl looked up, "I said, NEXT!" Carol crossed over the log and stood in front of the desk. The girl's face was buried back in the file. She flipped through several pages without making a sound. Then she picked up a pen. "Name?"

"Carol, my name is Carol Morgan."

"Of course it is," the young girl said as she began to write.

"Who are you?" Carol asked.

"Date of birth?"

"August 26, 2002".

The girl put down the file and stared into Carol's eyes. Something about her gaze was familiar. She looked like an angel, so soft and gentle. Carol reached out to touch her.

"Don't!" the young girl said. Her countenance quickly changed into something that triggered a deep fear in Carol's memory.

"Who are you?" Carol asked.

"What is your date of birth?" the young girl said through clenched teeth.

"I told you, August 26, 2002."

"No! On your bracelet! What is the date on your bracelet?"

Carol glanced at her wrist. She was shocked to see that the bracelet was back. *How'd that get there?* she wondered. She spun it around her wrist. Suddenly everything felt wrong. Her eyes darted around. "It's wrong. The date is wrong."

"What is it?" the girl demanded.

"December 29, 1937" Carol said, and then added, "But it's wrong!"

The girl picked up the file. She quickly flipped through several pages. Then she dropped the file on the desk. She placed both hands on the desk and said, "It's 2037, not 1937." She stared intently at Carol. "It doesn't matter. You're too early! It's not your time yet!"

Fear gripped Carol's heart as the young girl stood and leaned across the desk. The girl pointed and said, "You need to go back. You're too early. Come back when it's your time".

"Who are you?"

A sneer covered the young girl's face. She studied Carol for several intolerable seconds and then said, "Me? Who am I? Don't you recognize me, Carol? I'm your mother." With that the young girl broke into a maniacal laugh.

Carol turned and began running. The laughter seemed to echo through the trees. There was no escaping it. She ran back down the path as fast as she could. The laughter followed her. Up ahead she could see the end of the trail; beyond it was nothingness. She stopped at the very edge. *What do I do now?* Carol began turning in a small circle. She threw her hands into the air and screamed, "What am I supposed to do?"

"Carol!"

She stopped in her tracks.

"Carol Morgan! Can you hear me Carol?"

This is crazy!

"Can you hear me Carol?"

"Yes! Who are you? What am I supposed to do?"

"Wake up, Carol! Wake up!"

She bolted up. She was back in the middle of the long empty hallway. Her breath came in long deep gasps.

"Relax, Carol. Just relax. Everything's going to be alright," the voice assured her from the other side of the wall.

Several other voices started whispering at once.

"Is it time?"

"No. It's too soon. She's not ready."

"I think it's time. We can't wait any longer."

"There's too much at stake!"

"The transfer rate is still too weak."

"The memories have to take root before we disconnect."

"If we don't do it now we're going to lose her!"

"Remember what happened to the others."

Finally a familiar voice said, "Carol, how do you feel?"

Carol was confused. She closed her eyes. In her mind she could see the beautiful meadow again. She could see the young girl running towards her. She gritted her teeth, prepared for the worst—but something was different. The young girl was smiling and laughing as she ran towards her. Deep inside Carol's mind a memory was desperately trying to surface. Then it happened. The young girl cried out, "Mommy!"

Carol opened her eyes.

"How do you feel, Carol?" the voice asked again.

"Fine. I'm fine. Where's my daughter?"

Cheers and laughter erupted from the other side of the hall.

The familiar voice said, "Its time."

The lights in the hall began to fade. As darkness enveloped her, the walls seemed to melt away. A warm liquid embraced her. Carol felt at peace. She relaxed and let it happen. A soft light begin to surround her. Gradually she noticed shapes. There were people standing around her. She couldn't quite make them out. Her hair floated across the front of her face. She was encased in an amber colored liquid. Carol felt herself drifting.

"Relax, Carol. Let it happen".

She heard a sound overhead. Soft whispers gave way to animated conversations. She couldn't quite make out the words. She could feel the liquid draining around her. Its warmth was quite soothing. Light filled the room. Clarity came to her. She was lying on her back in a long glass tube. She felt something grab her ankles as the glass tube slid away from her. Suddenly she was surrounded by a team of doctors. A flurry of activity erupted around her. Through the chatter and the noise she could hear a young girl calling out, "Mommy! Are you alright Mommy?"

The familiar voice said, "Yes, honey. She's going to be fine." He wrapped his arm around the little girl and walked her beside the table. "Carol, do you know who this is?"

"That's my daughter, Tabitha. Are you okay sweetheart?"

"I missed you, Mommy!" Tabitha shrieked.

Carol looked at the man. "What happened?"

"There was a terrible accident. And this little girl saved your life."

Carol reached out for her daughter.

"They said I got to be your Mommy! Isn't that funny Mommy? Isn't that funny? I'm a Mommy too!"

"What are you talking about sweetheart?"

The familiar voice said, "There will be plenty of time for answers."

Carol didn't care. She held her daughter's hand. Nothing else mattered. One thing did trouble her, though. She looked back up at the familiar voice and asked, "What happened on December 29, 2037?"

Before he could answer, Tabitha said, matter-of-factly, "That's the day you died Mommy."

101

Carol's mind was swirling. Panic seized her. Nothing made sense. She was desperately looking for a mental hook to hang this bizarre experience on. She pulled her daughter close. It's not every day that you wake up to discover you're the world's first successful daughter-mother clone.

-8-

-Eat Your Peas-

"God is in heaven, and thou upon earth:
therefore let thy words be few."
Ecclesiastes 5:2

*This was my first attempt at writing a "101 word story." It was very
challenging to force myself to be so succinct.*

I t's not his fault. You really can't blame him. His parents, after all, were crazy. All that time chained in the basement. The screaming and beatings. All because he wouldn't eat his peas. Who eats peas anyway?

No, it's not his fault. But he'll show them. One day he'll escape. He'll be in charge. This dream comforts him.

He plays it over and over in his mind. They're old, feeble and weak. He shovels spoon after spoon into their mouths. Green goo is everywhere. "Now, now," he says, "Eat your peas." Then adds with a maniacal smile, "They're good for you."

-9-

-Terror-

"It takes few words to tell the truth"
Chief Joseph

This was my second attempt at writing a "101 word story." I wanted to see if I could write a horror/thriller with so few words.

Gasping. Running. Terror.

Darkness. He's coming! Faster! Faster! *Get out of here!*

Panic. Racing through the forest; laughter from behind. Falling, crawling, whimpering on the ground.

He's closer. Taunting. Mocking.

Becky, Ted, Danny—all dead. Must get up! Must run! Must escape!

Gasping, screaming, bolting awake. *Where am I? What's happening?*

Scanning the room. Shadows flicker. Awareness. *The cabin! A dream? Was it all a dream?*

Heart pounding. Silence. Deafening silence.

What's that sound?

Something sharp dragging along the floor. Soft chuckle outside the door. Clawing. Scratching. Laughter.

Cracking explosion. *An axe?*

He whispers, "Time to join your friends!"

-A Dog Named Lucky-

"If you want to imagine the future, imagine a boy and his dog and his friends. And a summer that never ends."
Neil Gaiman

I still remember the first time I saw him. He was just a puppy. A pretty small one at that. "Make sure he doesn't have big paws," my dad advised. He surmised that large paws were the sure signs of a puppy that was destined to be a very large dog. One look in his eyes and the size of his paws didn't matter to me at all. I had fallen in love, maybe for the first time.

He was basically a white dog covered with large brown and tan splotches. His tail had been bobbed off, or perhaps he was born that way. I never really knew. By his markings, you would have guessed that he had boxer in his blood. One look at the face and you knew you were dealing with a full-blood mutt. "A Heinz Fifty-Seven!" my dad declared. By that he meant that the dog was a mixture of a multiple of unknown breeds. I couldn't care less. I wasn't looking for a pedigree. I was looking for a friend. There was no doubt in my young mind that I had found one.

"Lucky," I said. "I'm gonna call him Lucky." And so it was. Lucky and I became inseparable in the early 1970's. We lived in a very rural area off of Bayou Liberty Road, just outside Slidell, Louisiana. Civilization seemed to have forgotten about us. That was just fine with me.

Lucky, as it turned out, proved to be anything but. He had several brushes with death. He was run over by the propane truck once. We didn't have natural gas back then. On the side of our house was a very large, silver tank that needed to be refilled every couple of months. It also served as a makeshift horse, when I was especially bored.

I watched the propane man fill our tank with some fascination. In my young, vivid imagination, he was refueling a rocket ship. I stood patiently by, waiting for him to leave so that I could ride it to the stars. As soon as he unhooked and wrapped up his hoses, I climbed into the cockpit (at least in my mind). Countdown started as he drove away. I was lost in my fantasy world. I should have been paying closer attention.

Lucky decided it was his job to chase the wheeled intruder away. He barely got to the end of our driveway when I was jerked out of my mission by the shrieking cries of a wounded dog. The driver never noticed what happened. He just shifted gears and kept going. I leapt down and ran to Lucky's side. The tire had apparently gone right over his midsection. He was in terrible agony. Against his wishes, I cradled Lucky in my arms and carried him to the house.

My mom helped me make a small bed for him in the pump shed. He looked pitiful. He could barely move. "What can we do?" I asked. I knew a trip to the vet was out of the question. These were hard times for our family. There was no extra money for anything as frivolous as a Vet visit for a mutt like Lucky. I cried as I imagined his pending demise.

For the entire day, Lucky didn't move at all. It wasn't looking good for him. When my dad got home, he followed me to the pump shed. He surveyed the damage and shook his head. He didn't candy coat it all. "I don't think he's gonna make it Sam," he said. My name, by the way, isn't Sam. It was a nickname that my grandpa tagged me with, for reasons known only to him. He even had a little ditty he would sing about it sometimes. "Sam, Sam, the ape man. Took a shit in the frying pan." He would smile and chuckle as he sang it. I know he meant it as a term of endearment. It just always struck me as strange. It was not common at all for my dad to call me Sam. Mostly he just called me "Boy". As in, "Boy do this" or "Boy grab that" or "Boy go feed the animals". "Boy" always seemed to be followed with a chore. I never perked up when I heard it. Maybe that's why, this time, he called me "Sam".

For the next two days, I nursed Lucky as best I could. He wouldn't eat or drink. He just laid there. If I tried to move him, he would whimper and whine. Against all odds, by the third day he got to his feet. Within a week, there was no sign at all of the accident. He was his normal self, running and playing; following me wherever I went.

Having Lucky was a godsend. You see, I lived on a dead-end shelled road, named "Reis Lane". I was always told that my mom's dad had built the road. Yet, for reasons I never knew, it was named after one of my uncles. There were a couple of other families on the street at that time. Our immediate neighbors were the Lapicolas. I was so excited when they moved in. My excitement quickly turned to disappointment when I realized that they didn't have any boys in the family. I didn't care much for girls back then. Those feelings would eventually change, but for the moment, I didn't have much use for them. After all, I was surrounded by them. I had five sisters of my own. My Aunt Ro and Uncle Bum were two houses up the road from us. They had six girls in their family. They did have two boys. One, my cousin Toot, was a full four years older than me. Once he discovered girls, I was on my own. The only other boy was his young brother, Ricky. I was nine years older. We really didn't hang out a whole lot back then.

Lucky seemed to even things out for me. He became my best friend. We played together every single day. Whenever I would try my hand at fishing, he would sit patiently beside me. I'll never forget the first time I jerked a small perch out of our duck pond. I pulled it so hard that it went sailing through the air behind me. It flew completely off the hook. It hit the ground, about fifteen feet behind me, flopping for dear life. I threw my cane pole down and ran to retrieve it. I had no plans of keeping it. I was just going to throw it back in the pond in order to catch it again another day. Lucky beat me to the fish. Before I could say anything, he snatched it between his teeth and chomped down. The fish immediately stopped moving. I stared at him in disbelief. I'd never seen a dog do anything like that before. Without a second's hesitation, he tore into that perch and devoured it. I was so surprised that I just looked at him and burst out laughing. It was the start of a new game. A very, very strange game. Lucky would wait patiently for my bobber to go under. He would jump up and run behind me, waiting for any wayward perch that might be sent his way. Sometimes, on purpose, more often than not, on accident, he would get his wish. I thought it was the craziest thing. I loved that dog.

Lucky's second serious encounter with tragedy was a mysterious one. For some reason, he got deathly sick. He was throwing up all over the place. He could barely walk straight. He kept falling over, again and again. My dad decided that he must have eaten something bad. Whatever it was, it nearly killed him. He wouldn't, or couldn't eat for several days. I tried to give him some water and he desperately lapped it up, only to spew it right back out a few seconds later. After several days, I could see his ribs. He was emaciated. He lost the strength to stand. Whenever he tried, he would just wobble on his spindly legs until he fell over on his side.

Once again, my dad pronounced that it didn't look good. "He's not going to make it this time," he said with an air of confidence. *Thanks Dad.* Once again, somehow, Lucky rallied. It took a while, but he got his strength back. He fattened up and resumed his position as my ever-present sidekick.

During the long days of summer, I decided to teach him how to fetch a stick. He never understood the concept. He loved chasing any stick I would throw. He never, no not ever, brought one back. No matter how much I begged and pleaded. He just didn't seem to get the concept. It was frustrating to me. After all, I had seen dogs on TV happily trot sticks back to their owners. It looked like a fun game. One that I was eager to play with Lucky. I sat there watching him destroy yet another stick, with no intention of bringing it back to me, wondering what to do. A lightbulb went off in my head. I came up with a way to make him bring me the stick back. I grinned as I got my plan ready. I went inside and fetched my dad's rod-n-reel. I snipped the hook off and tied a stick in its place. I dangled the bizarre lure in front of Lucky. He got very excited. I drew back and cast it as far as I could. He had no idea what I was doing. The second he heard that stick land, he turned and raced for it.

I waited until he had it clinched between his teeth. I started reeling it in. The whole time I was saying, "Good boy! Come! Bring it back!" I practically had to drag him back the first couple of times. After about an hour, he eventually got it. He was running back to me with the stick faster than I could reel it in. I took a chance and removed it from the line. I looked at him. "Go get it boy!" I said. He bolted away as fast as he could when I threw the stick. It bounced on the ground. He snatched it up and started chewing on it. I was afraid I had been premature in cutting the stick free. I stood up and called out, with as much encouragement as I could, "Come! Bring it!" Lucky turned around and looked at me. I'll never forget that moment. Something clicked. He stopped what he was doing and ran straight back to me with the stick. He dropped it at my feet. I swooped him into my arms and smothered him with admiration. "Good boy! Good boy!" I said over and over. Lucky ate it up. He was so excited he couldn't stand still. He spun in a circle, looked up at me and barked. That was my signal. I hurled the stick as far as I could. He bolted to it. No sooner did he snatch it up, than he turned around and trotted it back to me. I was over the moon with excitement. I'm sure there are better ways to train a dog than with a rod-n-reel. But, I was just a kid, and this seemed to work just fine.

Sometime after that, I decided to expand Lucky's training. I had a squirrel tail hanging on the wall in my room. Why? Because I was boy who lived in the country, I suppose. At any rate, I used an ice pick to secure the tail, about three feet off the ground, on the large oak tree that stood in the center of our yard. At first, I stood right beside it and pointed at the tail. It already had Lucky's full attention. "Get it!" I said. It took several attempts before he ever seemed to understand what I wanted him to do. As soon as he snatched the tail, I grabbed him and smothered him with a heaping dose of "good boys."

After a few minutes, I stepped a little further from the tree and had him stand beside me. I pointed at the tail, "Get it!" I said. He ran back to the tree and snatched the tail. I was elated. I pressed my luck and moved about fifteen feet from the tree. I grabbed his collar and made him stand beside me. He seemed to know what I wanted. He turned back to look at the tail. I let go of his collar, to see if he would wait. He did. He stood patiently waiting for the command. "Get it!" I said. He shot out from beside me and ran to retrieve the tail. I laughed my head off. I was so proud of him. Eventually, I worked us all the way back to the front steps of the house, probably forty feet from the tree. I sat on the steps and tried my best to act nonchalant. Lucky sat beside me. He seemed to be content. He was just happy to be playing. After a few moments, I pointed back at the tail. "Get it!" I said. He leapt to his feet and raced back to the tree. I had stuck the tail up a little higher this time. He had to run up the tree a little bit to snatch the tail. It didn't hinder him in the least. He slowly trotted the tail back to me. He seemed to be just as proud as I was. It was a glorious moment. I often go back to it in my mind. I loved that dog.

We didn't live too far from Bayou Liberty. Sometimes, Lucky would follow my cousins and I on our walk to the bayou. We carried a couple of cane poles and what meager tackle we could scramble together. There was always an old rusty can filled with earthworms that we had scurried around in search of. Lucky would always sit patiently beside me, waiting for any scaled appetizers that might be flung in his direction. More often than not, our fishing trips quickly escalated into swimming trips. Lucky was as eager to hit the water as we were. He would splash and swim in the murky waters right beside us. This was why summer was invented. It was a carefree, fun-filled time of my life; made that way by a very peculiar mutt. I loved that dog. He meant everything to me. I wanted these days to last forever. Sadly, that would not be the case.

One day, near the end of the summer, I came outside and called for Lucky. No answer. That was odd. I called again. Nothing. I started searching for him. He was nowhere to be found. My mom said he was probably just off somewhere exploring. I left it at that. Evening came and went with no sign of Lucky. The next day was the same. I called in vain. He never came. I looked everywhere I could think to, but I couldn't find him anywhere. I was devastated. I had no idea what happened to him. My dad said he probably ran away. *Thanks, Dad.* That hurt to think about. Why would Lucky run away from me? We were pals. What could I have done to chase him away? Maybe he's lost? Maybe, knowing Lucky, he had gotten hit by a car and was laying somewhere, hurt, waiting for me to help him. These thoughts haunted my young dreams. Days passed by with no sign of Lucky. I was in the first major funk of my life. I was devastated. My dog, my best friend, was gone.

Before I knew it, school started back. I went through the motions. August gave way to September, and in no time, I was absorbed in the social activities of the school year. The months ticked by. I had given up all hope of ever seeing Lucky again. Christmas came and went. The routine of school, homework, and chores seemed to cause the days to tick by in a rapid succession. Before I knew it, I was looking at the end of another school year. It seemed like a lifetime ago since I had last seen Lucky. I guessed those days were gone forever. Summer was coming and I was excited about that, till I remembered that it would be a summer without Lucky.

On one day, in particular, my mom was driving us back home. She said she needed to stop at a friend's house first. She pulled into a rural area behind Bayou Bonfouca. It was about three or four miles from our house. She pulled alongside the road in front of the house. "You want to come in?" she asked. I just shook my head. She left me to wait in the truck.

I sat in the truck, fiddling with whatever I could find, trying to stave off boredom. After a few minutes, a flash of something in the side mirror caught my attention. I focused my attention on it, happy to have something to do. I could clearly see all the way down to the end of the block. I leaned forward. I watched a small dog running around the front of someone's yard. He was about a half a block away. There was something very familiar in its movements. My heart started beating rapidly as I noticed its markings. It was basically a white dog, covered with brown and tan splotches. *Could it be?* I wondered. I watched the dog for several minutes. I was afraid to hope that it might be Lucky. What were the odds? We were several miles from our house. Plus the only way to get here was to cross an old single lane bridge. It couldn't be Lucky. *Right?* I had to know for sure. I popped the door open and stepped out of the truck.

I faced the direction of the dog and continued to watch him. He was running around by the end of a driveway. I felt foolish, but I had to make sure. So I cupped my hands beside my mouth and hollered out, "Lucky!" The dog froze. It turned its face towards me. Even from that distance, it seemed that our eyes locked. The second they did, all of my doubts were removed. It was Lucky!

He didn't hesitate. He took off like a flash of lightening, running straight for me. I couldn't breathe. *This must be a dream*, I thought. I was smiling ear to ear. The closer he got, it seemed the faster he ran. I dropped down to my knees just as he reached me. Lucky leapt into my arms. He was as excited as I was. He started licking my face all over. I held him in my arms, laughing and crying simultaneously. I had given up all hope of ever seeing him again. And, now, here he was in my arms. All was right in the universe again. I loved that dog.

Even at that young age, I remember thinking how random the

universe was. If I hadn't been with my mom, if she hadn't decided to stop off at her friend's house, if I hadn't decided to just wait in the truck—I would have missed this magical moment. One day would have blended into the next and I would have missed my one chance to be reunited with Lucky. I held him as tight as I could. He was jumping all over the place. I finally just sat on the ground and petted him. I felt so much love in that moment.

I decided to surprise my mom. I got back in the truck and Lucky automatically followed me. I moved him down to the floorboard in front of me. I didn't want her to see him until after she was in the truck. I watched her finally come out of her friend's house. I was giddy with excitement. I couldn't wait for her to see Lucky.

She opened the door and absentmindedly slid in. She looked down at Lucky in absolute shock. "Is that your dog?" she asked.

I ran my fingers across the top of his head. "Yes!" I said. "It's Lucky! I found Lucky!"

My mom was excited, but something seemed to be bothering her. "Where did he come from?" she asked.

Who cares? I thought. "I saw him playing down the block. I called his name and he came running."

She turned around and stared down the block. "Was he in somebody's yard?" she asked.

What is she getting at? I wondered. "Yeah, that last house on the end of the street. He was in their driveway." I studied her face. "Why? What difference does that make?" I asked.

"Don't you think we should go knock on their door? See if it's their dog?" she asked.

I couldn't believe what I was hearing. "No!" I practically shouted. "It's NOT their dog. It's Lucky. He's MY dog!" I was suddenly afraid that I was about to lose Lucky once again. "I'm not giving him back. He's my dog, not theirs."

114

My mom wasn't convinced that we should just drive away. She saw how determined I was and finally relented. She started the truck up and we drove away. I breathed a sigh of relief. However, she turned the truck around and made her way back towards that house. I panicked. *She couldn't. She wouldn't*, I thought. She slowed down as we passed the house. She glanced over to see if anyone was outside. Not seeing anyone, she kept driving. I let out a long breath. I reached down and pulled Lucky up into my lap. I held him as tight as I could. I really loved that dog. I never wanted to lose again. Sadly, our reunion was going to be a very short one.

When we got home, I forgot about whatever homework or chores I had to do. I spent the rest of the day playing with Lucky. He fetched sticks and chased me all around the yard. It was a wonderful day. My dad couldn't believe it when he saw Lucky. "Hmm," he said. "I just figured he was dead." *Thanks Dad.*

The next morning, I played with Lucky a few minutes before heading to catch the bus. All day long I thought about how great it was having him back. I couldn't believe my good fortune. I waited in agony for the school day to end. I wanted to get home and play with my dog. We had a lot of catching up to do. It was going to be a great summer. Sadly, I was wrong about that.

Lucky was waiting for me when I got home. He ran and greeted me. I had missed him so much. As soon as I walked in the house, to put my stuff away, something didn't feel right. The way my mom was looking at me spelled trouble. She was standing in the hallway with the phone in her hand. "Here he is now," she said. I held my breath.

"What?" I whispered.

She placed her hand over the phone. "This lady would like to speak to you about your dog."

"No!" I said out loud. She probably heard me, but I didn't care. "It's my dog. I'm not giving him back!"

"Nobody's asking you to give him back. She just wants to talk to you. You owe her that. She took care of him for you."

I had a hard knot in my stomach. I didn't like this one bit. I hated to agree, but I knew my mom was right. I should at least thank her taking care of Lucky for me. I shuffled towards her and grudgingly took the phone. I took a deep breath. "Hello," I muttered.

The kindest voice I think I've ever heard responded from the other end of the line. "Hello, Sweetie," she said. I don't remember all the details of our conversation. I was too numb, too scared. Basically, she had been worried sick about the dog. She was so afraid that it had run off or gotten injured. She was happy to hear that the dog was safe with me; that we were reunited. She then asked me for a favor. Would I be willing to bring the dog by so she could say goodbye? Everything within me wanted to say "No. No way!" Instead, I sheepishly said, "Yes mam. That sounds okay."

I was gut sick. I didn't like where I thought this was going. She sounded like a saintly old lady. She was practically crying on the phone. She had been so worried about the dog. She hadn't slept much last night worrying about him. When she couldn't find him, she started knocking on her neighbor's doors. Hoping that maybe someone had seen him. When she got to my mom's friend, she had her answer.

We drove to her house in silence. I held Lucky in my lap the whole way there. "I'm not giving him back," I told my mom as we pulled into her driveway.

"He's your dog," she said. "You do what you think's best."

I slowly got out of the truck. Lucky followed me. This time, it was my mom who stayed in the truck and waited for me. I let out a deep sigh. I walked up the steps to her and knocked on the door. Lucky stood beside me. "Come in," I heard someone say in the voice of everyone's beloved grandmother. I opened the door and let myself in. Lucky pushed around me and rushed into the house. This wasn't a strange place to him.

An elderly woman was sitting in a large chair. Lucky made a beeline for her. Her eyes lit up and she started crying. He was all over her. He was licking and greeting her the same way he did me. I couldn't hardly

116

stand to watch. It just felt wrong. The old lady held Lucky's face in her hand. She started kissing him. "Missy," she said. "Oh, Missy, I was so afraid."

Missy? I wondered, *who the hell is Missy?* I wanted to be angry at the old lady. I really did. As far as I was concerned, she stole my dog. As I watched them love one another, however, a new emotion rose up in me. Compassion. My dog or not, I felt horrible for breaking the old lady's heart.

She invited me to sit down. She thanked me profusely for bringing Missy by. I wanted to correct her, but decided against it. "Missy was a godsend to us," she said.

Us? I wondered. As far as I could tell, she was alone.

She wiped fresh tears from her eyes. "Well, really, she was a godsend to my husband," she said. She raised a handkerchief to her eyes and wiped them. "He passed away last month," she said. Fresh tears flowed down her face.

Great! I thought. *Now I really feel horrible.*

She composed herself and leaned back in her chair. "He had cancer," she said.

Why are you telling me this? I wondered.

"He got so depressed. He didn't have anything to live for anymore," she said. More tears spilled from her eyes. She didn't bother wiping them away. "He found Missy by the side of the road. She was in the ditch. Somebody had hit her and just left her there to die."

That sounds like Lucky, I thought.

"He brought her home and nursed that dog back to life. He did," she said. The memory brought a smile to her face. "Lil Missy gave him a reason to live again." She rubbed Lucky's head. "Yes you did, girl, didn't you?" She stared into Lucky's eyes a few seconds and asked, "You miss him too, don't you?" The way Lucky buried his face in her lap, he seemed to understand what she was saying.

She looked up at me and essentially said the same thing I'd said so many times over the last couple of years. "He loved this dog."

Now I was crying. I couldn't help it.

"After he was gone," she said, as she stared out the window, "Missy was all I had left. The thought of losing her was more than I could handle." She looked back to me. I had never felt such compassion and love for a total stranger. "When I'm with Missy, it feels like he's still here with me," she said. "You understand, don't you?" she asked me.

I nodded my head. I wasn't really sure if I did or not. The only thing I really understood, was that I was about to lose my dog again. This time would be different though. This time it would be me walking away from him. The thought of it was tearing me apart. We stared at each other for a few moments in shared silence. In those moments, I think we understood and appreciated each other's pain.

I could tell she was struggling with something she wanted to ask me. Perhaps she didn't feel like she had the right to ask, but her pain was so deep, her loss was so fresh, that she finally asked. I already knew what the question was going to be. I also, already knew what my answer would be.

"Do you think, you could, maybe let me keep Missy a bit longer?" she asked. She lowered her head. I wasn't sure if she was ashamed to ask so much of me, a total stranger, or if she was afraid I would say no. What boy would ever willingly give up his dog?

It took all the strength my young heart could muster. I glanced over on the coffee table. A portrait of her husband stared back at me. The words that came out of my mouth came straight from my heart. I think they bypassed my brain all together. "Yes," I whispered. "I think that would be alright." Tears were streaming down my face. I could barely breathe. I knew that "a little bit longer" actually meant forever. I would never see Lucky again.

She held out her arms to me. I walked into them and we embraced. Lucky/Missy pressed between us. I knew that the pain I was feeling had to be much less than what she was going through. The love and compassion I felt for her seemed to merge with the love I felt for Lucky. His love and companionship had meant so much to me. My love for Lucky would be my gift to her.

There was some solace, even in my young heart, to understand that my loss would bring much comfort to her. I was okay with that. In the end, I felt like I wasn't really losing Lucky. I was sharing him with someone who needed him even more than I did.

After we had said all we could say on the matter, she thanked me again, from the bottom of her heart. I was doing my best to say goodbye to Lucky. She suddenly had a thought, "Hey," she said, "When Missy has puppies, you can have the pick of the litter." I guess she thought that would cheer me up. It didn't. All it did was make me realize that she would be keeping Lucky forever. And, I really didn't have the heart to tell her that "Missy" was a boy. "She" wouldn't be having puppies anytime soon.

I stood at the door to leave. I wiped my tears on my sleeve. Then I looked at Lucky one last time. It was the last time I ever saw him. He looked so happy with the old lady. He seemed to know that this was his home now. It was his job to comfort her. He looked up at me, for the last time. I wondered if he knew. There was a depth to his eyes I hadn't noticed before. *This is the right thing to do*, I told myself. That sure didn't make it any easier.

I walked back out to the truck in silence. I just stared out the window as my mom backed out of the driveway. I thought it odd that she didn't ask me where Lucky was. She knew, before I did, that I would be giving my dog to this dear old woman. She knew this had been a very difficult thing for me to do. When she finally spoke, she said, "Son, if you don't do another good deed the rest of your life, I think this one, by itself, will probably get you into heaven."

Her words were of little comfort to me in the moment. My heart was too numb to hear them. I've thought about them as the years have come

119

and gone. I'll be honest, I don't know if there even is a heaven. But, if there is, I'm certain that Lucky is already there. Hopefully, he'll be the first one to greet me when it's my time to cross over.

11

-Conversion-

"…anyone who belongs to Christ has become a new person. The old life
is gone; a new life has begun."
St. Paul, II Corinthians 5:17

*As a young man, I tried, as best as I could, to find my own way. I wanted
to know the truth about God; about life. This poem was an early attempt
at expressing those longings. Finding my own path has been a lifelong
journey; one that continues to this day.*

Into an abyss of death and gloom,
I descend most eagerly;
unaware of my own impending doom.

The fires do laughingly beckon me down,
to the bottom of the abyss,
where only death is found.

My skin completely scorched
and my fate surely set;
my body now succumbs
to the flame's fiery net.

Only now do I realize
that surely I shall die.
Yet, my heart,
reluctantly, ponders why

In a fit of despair,
I retrieve my sight.
Straining to see,
I notice a light.

Mysteriously beckoning me with love;

JOHN ALBERT

I marvel, even more,
at the sight above.

Straining my ears,
so that I might hear,
the light speaks, saying,
"Come, draw near."

"Open your heart
and arise from your sleep.
Walk now the straight,
instead the steep."

I turn and scream
as the fire lashes at me.
Here and now I decide
my new destiny.

My heart pouring forth
with will and might,
I reach out my hand
and grasp the light.

I touch only the hem
of the light's outer glide,
and instantly
it draws me near to its side.

Now safe in the arms
and love of the light,
I have found my peace,
both day and night.

Looking down at the fire,
I feel reassured.
Where once I was dead,
now am I cured.

12

-A Life in a Day-

"Life's but a walking shadow, a poor player, that struts and frets his hour upon the stage, and then is heard no more; it is a tale told by an idiot, full of sound and fury, signifying nothing."
William Shakespeare

I wrote this poem when I was seventeen years old. I had joined the Army and was away from home for the first time. Like most teenagers, I wrestled with angst and found myself in an existential crisis. This was my attempt to put words to those feelings.

Yesterday, I was born.
For reasons not known,
I was given life.
Born into a world of hatred, deceit and death.

In the morning I grew.
I rapidly learned of love;
how to have fun;
how to enjoy life.

At noon, I learned aggression, deceit, and hatred.
I learned how to hate my means of entry into this world.
I learned how to steal and to kill.
I learned how to deceive my friends
and become an enemy.
I learned how to adjust.

In the evening, I remembered.
I remembered my hour of birth.
I remembered my discovery of love.
I thought of my minutes spent chasing the wind.

I remembered the seconds I used for laughing,
and the minute I cried.
I remembered how I learned to hate.
I remembered the times I used for
deceit and thievery.
I pondered the seconds
occupied in lust,
and the time I lost in vain projects.

In the night, I cried.
I saw my day as a puff of smoke;
my ideas as vain.
I realized my anguish,
and I prayed.

Today, I died.

13

-One Single Stage-

"The earth is a very small stage in a vast, cosmic arena."
Carl Sagan

I wrote this poem after reading Carl Sagan's 'Pale Blue Dot'. I was so moved by his book, that I purchased the picture of earth the Voyager I spacecraft took. It shows our planet from a distance of four billion miles. Earth appears as a tiny blue dot floating in the vastness of space. I hung the picture in my office, over my computer. It was a humble reminder of my place in the universe.

When I think of the earth
as a single stage;
I see our great God
in a balcony seat,
scores of Angels at God's feet.

No spoken word,
no deed,
no thought,
escapes the notice of the heavenly loft.

My steps are ordered.
My way made right.
My life is surrounded
by God's holy light.

I exist for God,
God exists for me,
on this solitary stage of eternity.

My faith is adequate,
for I know the limit,
of the entire universe
and the God within it.

But what if this stage is just one among many?
A speck of sand on a beach of infinity?

When the cosmos extend
beyond my sense of sight,
is my God still God
beyond those distant points of light?

ABOUT THE AUTHOR

John Albert, a Louisiana native, is a retired US Army Officer. He lives on the beautiful Gulf Coast with his lovely wife, Ann. They share their home with Boudreaux and Thibodaux; two rambunctious schnauzers.

Albert, a sometime pirate, optimistic gardener, beer and cigar aficionado, and avid dad-dancer, enjoys writing while listening to the sounds of the waves and the wind whisper through the pine trees. His other published works can be found on Amazon.

41217216R00083

Made in the USA
Lexington, KY
06 June 2019